"A SMALL CLASSIC . . . MAY BE PRICE'S MOST INVITING NOVEL."

USA Today

"[Price is] a master of narrative voices, developing them with unswerving confidence and concentration."

The Washington Post

"Those shopping for a philosophy of life could do no better than to look to the works of Reynolds Price. . . . [A] hypnotic tale of loss and redemption."

Time

"[An] intelligent and very satisfying novel . . . THE TONGUES OF ANGELS is graciously formal, and highly appropriate for its fused central themes of art, faith and memory."

Chicago Tribune

THE TONGUES OF ANGELS

REYNOLDS PRICE

BALLANTINE BOOKS • NEW YORK

Library of Congress Catalog Card Number: 89-37427

ISBN: 0-345-37102-X

This edition published by arrangement with Atheneum Publishers, an Imprint of Macmillan Publishing Company.

Manufactured in the United States of America

First Ballantine Books Edition: May 1991

FOR

KATHRYN WALKER

AND

JAMES TAYLOR

O N E

I'M AS PEACEFUL A MAN AS YOU'RE LIKELY TO MEET IN America now, but this is about a death I may have caused. Not slowly over time by abuse or meanness but on a certain day and by ignorance, by plain lack of notice. Though it happened thirty-four years ago, and though I can't say it's haunted my mind that many nights lately, I suspect I can draw it out for you now, clear as this noon. I may need to try.

I was twenty-one, an official man. I could almost surely have held him back; he deserved to stay. It wouldn't have taken a hero to do it, just a person with more common sense than I had at the time and, as I said, more attention to things. Half the mistakes I've made till now are mistakes of attention. I haven't really watched or I watched too close. And the only consolation I've had, for his death at least, is the hope that I learned a necessary lesson and that—from his short life, short not small—I made a part of the work I've done.

I'm a painter, of pictures not houses. From the time I started, back before grade school and down till now, everything I paint tries to look like the world, not just the world behind my eyes. And since I've been lucky and determined enough to support myself with mainly representational pictures, right through the abstract expressionist years, I've used the place and hour of his death a good many times—the actual air and light of that evening.

IT HAPPENED THE SUMMER OF 1954 AT A BOYS' CAMP IN the Great Smoky Mountains of North Carolina. I was a counselor there for ten weeks between my third and fourth years of college. He was a camper, age fourteen—Raphael Noren. That was two syllables, pronounced RAY-*field* with the *d* silent. Fourteen was the oldest you could be at Camp Juniper, pending a dispensation in the event of arrested development. All this was two decades before the nutritional boom of the postwar years excited all the hormonal clocks and made us a nation of sexually precocious giants. But even back then, after age fourteen you were too hot to handle and likely to be more of a bad influence than not.

Rafe was a lot of things; but whatever else, he was not a bad influence. Not intentionally, not on boys his own age. He laid down around him, and several steps ahead, the grave and pleasing air of a generous heart. Most children look out, grab a sight or two, run home and think about what it means for *them*. Rafe was the only outward-looking child I ever knew or heard of. Somehow he felt safe enough to watch the world. One way or other, everybody felt that trait as somehow unnerving. And we all responded according to our natures. A surprising lot of Rafe's elders laughed. Though they couldn't admit it, he was plainly too grown. But the one thing nobody did was ignore him.

Rafe's draw worked in all directions, and that too came from his watchful ways. Very few people think that they've been noticed enough, and they almost always rise to the bait. They tend to think it means you like them. And Rafe was all but factory-set to believe the best about everybody and everything. Not that he liked everything he saw. But if you were human, Rafe hoped he could please or at least amuse you. And besides his face, he'd already got his grown man's voice. It was a substantial baritone with none of the hints of embryonic preacher, politician or other fund-raiser that some boys get with premature manhood. It helped him a lot.

His face was also well advanced in its walk towards the uncluttered dignity it might have had at forty. And though his body was still supported on the compact bones of childhood, he was taller than his age—maybe five foot nine— and the skin of his calves and lower belly had grown the gold hair of first manhood. I'd grown it myself, only seven years before. But young as I was, I could already see it wearing away on my ankles and losing the metallic luster that makes you feel more like some brand of ram with gold fleece than a helpless boy.

Rafe was so far ahead of most boys his age that he seemed a little pained at the institutional Saturday night mass shower jamborees. We counselors were supposed to make them sound like major entertainment events. But of course they were just a stab at insuring one bath per week for the many reluctant. I never thought Rafe was embarrassed for him-

self; he worried about the others. They'd fix on his plumb-
ing with helpless amazement. And the key to their feeling
was, nobody laughed. I suspect he thought his precocity
would shame them and he hated that. Since one of his surprising qualities was wit—most of the good-looking young
people I've met have all the wit of a basement door—he at
first tried to joke about it in public.

At the first jamboree of his session, for instance, when
Rafe saw them staring, he stretched his member to its limit,
strummed it like a banjo and sang "You Are My Sun-
shine." But he must have seen that it saddened the other
boys, like standing by helpless at a vandal act. From then
out anyhow he took a far corner and kept himself hid. Better
samples of his wit will surface later. But I need at the start
to warn you against rejecting him early as a sober saint.
That he was not. Any hour in Rafe's presence would let you
see a dozen ways in which he was still a boy. But what I
ask you to see at the start is something difficult. For surprising lengths of time most days, Rafe Noren showed
stretches of majesty. And everybody around him knew it,
not just the painter in residence, me.

In republican America, majesty's a trait seen mostly in
photographs of Yosemite Valley or statues of Lincoln; so
I'm hard put to give you parallel examples. Imagine a tall
girl stepping towards you from a Botticelli "Spring" with
your name on her lips, not knowing she's grander than the
life all around. Or try thinking of a tall lean diver who
honors the air turning down, slow motion, from a ten-meter
board and vanishes sooner than you might hope. Or the
eighteen-year-olds on ancient Greek tombstones. They wave
you in with what may be the start of a smile towards absolute rest.

* * *

BUT I'VE RUN WAY AHEAD. RAFE NOREN WON'T APPEAR
for some time yet. I need to explain what brought me near
him and why I may have a part in his ending. Like all real
stories, this one starts with my parents. They had excellent
practical sense but were not highly educated. My father was
denied college by a lack of family money, the last of eight
children. Mother stayed at home because girls then mostly
did, but also her parents died before she was sixteen. Father
had aimed to be a civil engineer; Mother dreamed of being
an actress.

That may have made them too generous with me, who
was their only child. So I have to admit that I got through
my first twenty years without ever holding a real job. I made
little pieces of money here and there by mowing yards,
refinishing furniture and drawing portraits of children and
dogs. But summers were mine for loafing, reading, playing
with friends and dodging polio. Those were the standard
dreamy times, much written about and featured in movies,
when middle-class children in green suburbs invented their
lazy heedless way, minus money and jobs, between their
well-behaved winters in school.

And the reason I got a job when I did had nothing to do
with virtue or vigor. My father had died the previous winter, the kind of heart attack that downs you in the midst of
trying to phone your wife and say goodbye. And that was
followed by more than a week of lingering agony with con-
gestive heart failure. Mother and I weren't penniless yet;
but three weeks after we buried Father, she took a job in
an office supply store. And I saw that if I really was going
to seize my fate and study in Europe after I finished college,

then I'd better put shoulder to wheel as well and see if it moved.

Even in 1954 there weren't many jobs for clean white boys with slim common sense and no practical experience. In the late winter as I was beginning to worry, Mother's minister came up with a letter from Albert Jenkins, a famous youth leader and founder-owner of old Camp Juniper up beyond Asheville. In those days the North Carolina mountains were strewn with camps—all firmly segregated as to gender and race, though few of us noticed the fact that early. They were generally named for things Indian or things in nature. And none was more highly regarded than Juniper.

A few weeks later "Chief" Jenkins, maybe sixty, spent an evening in Winston and met with a small group of young men like me in search of an easy summer's work in no more than semiwild conditions with pay so low that it seemed Errol-Flynn-buccaneering of Jenkins to state his case. But of course he did, from just below the pulpit of our Presbyterian church, to three dozen men more or less my age one later winter evening.

This is pretty nearly what he said. "I like to think that, for whichever ones of you are earnest tonight and meet our standards for ten weeks at Juniper, you won't be working but reaping a harvest of lifelong gifts—three fine meals a day, your bunk in a cabin with boys whose minds you're expected to inspire, thrilling religious and musical programs, Indian dancing, woodcraft training, all our entertainment facilities, one day a week off to visit Asheville or climb in the mountains for your spiritual needs and as a token of my personal thanks—three hundred and thirty dollars on the final day."

Even in 1954, $330 for ten weeks of six-day round-the-clock work was less than joke pay. And when there was a dazed pause between the preposterous offer and the interviews, half of the candidates slumped their shoulders and melted up the aisles. For practical reasons I should have joined them; I needed a lot more money than that. But whether it was the blindness of immediate despair or a sudden fascination with the old man's heat, light and gall, I was one of the six who stayed.

I'd grown up in a wide spectrum of Protestant churches, from the chilled Presbyterians through the sweaty fervor of Tar River Baptists through the politer Methodists and on out to pasture. So I was more than familiar with the generation of clear-eyed thigh-squeezing ex-YMCA types who populated the church and youth field. No denomination was safe. But Chief Jenkins blazed like a nova in their firmament.

He was ramrod straight in a Spartan chair when I entered the preacher's study. The only vacant chair almost touched his. He waved me towards it and gave me the first of his shot-down smiles—an instant grin on ivory false teeth; then an instant end, as if shot down. Another trait of the youth-leader class in those trusting days was a tendency to proximity. They were hell-bent to crowd you and *press the flesh*, in Lyndon Johnson's perfect phrase of a decade later. It seemed your flesh was a fuel they needed. They'd rub your palm or the back of your neck or any other part you'd freely concede. I'd long since learned how to go glass-eyed and flaccid in their grip. It cooled their fires and they let you drop. So with Chief's ice-water pupils nailed on me, I took the chair, expecting at least a thigh massage.

I'd read him wrong. He was all but stone deaf and wouldn't admit it. Our meeting lasted maybe four minutes.

He said he'd heard of my father's death; was I now the man of the family?

I was.

He'd also heard I was on the college paper. Did that mean I qualified to edit *The Thunderbird*, the camp's mimeographed weekly?

I hoped it did.

I'd want to cover inspirational news and to make good efforts to use each boy's name once in the weeks he was present in camp. They hadn't taught art for a number of years in the crafts program, an early artist having died of diabetes after the annual watermelon feast. Would I like to organize a sketching class with real substance to it?

I didn't probe the word *substance* for fear it meant Bible illustrations, but I agreed in principle.

Chief drilled me a final stare in the eyes—today it would constitute assault. Then he jerked upright on spastic puppet joints. They were the clue to his other secret, which was bad arthritis. He asked if I'd wait outside with the others. And far from making a final grab, another common tactic, he seemed momentarily shocked when I offered a forthright parting handshake.

The last man came out a quarter hour later. All six of us were young enough to lapse into the dumb patience of youth, so we loosened our ties for the standard wait on the grown-ups. And the cockier three, not I, knocked together some easy jokes about the old guy. "What does he use when he nicks himself shaving?—Plastic Wood." But they laughed too soon.

In less than three minutes, Chief's door flew open; and the blue eyes bore down on us again. Precisely on me. We'd all stood up, to be sure. But with not one word of regret to the others, he rapped my tie at breastbone level—my brain felt the thud—and he said "*You're* my man. I'll write you a letter." With that he was gone, no farewell handshakes and not a dry crumb for the five stunned losers.

THAT CONFIRMED MY HUNCH. WILDER THAN EVER AND IN the teeth of a salary that was less than a tip—less than a fifth of what I could have made in construction work—I was bound to accept. I checked with Mother. All her life she saw no point in doing anything that was not your heart's hunger. And I'd inherited her tendency to impulsive choices; so of course she said if it's what I wanted, that was all she needed to hear—just *go*. A few days later when Chief's formal letter came, I signed on readily and added an acceptance that was more Pentecostal than I generally manage to be on paper. I didn't quite shout or speak in tongues, but I said something like "I promise you an abundant harvest for your trust in me." I had that glowing a view of myself, though only a Chief could make me admit it.

The time of my boyhood was a far more fervent time than many now believe. Today anybody whose eyes glint fire, and who sees himself as a gift to the world, is likely to be a flimflam man or an out-of-state strangler, maybe both. But don't forget, we boys born in the early 1930s had watched our parents body-surf the Depression and in some cases wipe out. We'd been too young to fight in the Second War but just old enough to hear the news and understand what an all-time evil genius had brought on the conflict. And we got a thrilling dose of patriotism and high moral expectation from our participation in scrap metal drives, old bacon grease drives (to grease shell casings), paper drives, war bonds.

In short we lived through the grandest long entertainment event in human history, with the gleamingest heroes and villains. Our standards for the future were immensely and rightly high. Show me a later villain with the black radiance of Hitler or brighter heroes than Roosevelt and Churchill. And the fact that not one of us had fired so much as a single live shot left us with high hopes of our own chance at grappling with a demon someday. Chief's eyes then had stirred that tender wound inside my mind. I've said it yearned for rousing touch and a call to action but maybe not then.

ANYHOW I NAVIGATED THE FINAL MONTHS OF MY CLASSES, concentrating less on my studies than on the manufacture of adequate reasons for not spending weekends at Mother's—she lived two hours from my dormitory room. I must have understood that I was beginning an effort to bury my father. To be sure, he was decently interred under gray Vermont granite, with vacancies beside him for Mother and me. Bury him in my life, I meant.

The sights I'd witnessed in his last few days are, to this day, the worst I've seen—and as an artist-journalist, I saw Vietnam. But even the sights don't begin to match the domino set of mental dilemmas. You are now the man at bat in your home, plus you've suddenly *got* the woman you envied him all your life. Nothing stands between you and her, except God of course and a Heavenly host with flaming swords. But that spring and summer, I was slaving full-time to blind myself to the fresh home movies that were scalding my mind. *Not* remembering my father meant not seeing Mother. I tried it, as I said, and she let me—to a point.

* * *

BUT I DID SPEND TEN DAYS AT HOME IN EARLY JUNE.
Mother left the house for work at eight-thirty every morning
and never got back before six. That freed me to sleep as
late as I wanted. Then I'd get up, slip on some old shorts
and draw or paint watercolors in the steamy yard. Or I'd
write the endless illustrated letters I was noted for among
my friends. I'd tell them my news, inch by inch, with semi-
comic marginal drawings. The sketches would burst now
and then into my equivalent of visual nuclear war, a careful
bird or flower they might want to frame or risk blaspheming
the Holy Ghost. It was what I could do that none of them
could, just that one thing; but they all seemed to like it.
After supper Mother and I would sit in the den and watch
the television that Father had introduced into the house only
two years before.

Those were the good days of Jackie Gleason and live
drama and of Liberace's epicene debut. A good index to my
father's kind nature lies in his first response to Liberace.
The three of us sat in dumbstruck silence through the whole
candlelit hour of the entertainer's TV debut. When it ended
I really couldn't guess my parents' reaction—their musical
taste ran to Fred Waring and his Pennsylvanians—but when
Mother rose to make more popcorn, Father looked at me
earnestly, "Son, couldn't something be done for him?" Not
with him, notice, but *for* him.

And there Mother and I sat through most of my ten nights
at home. We were a good way too far gone in life before
TV to become the instant zombies that most later Americans are, at a flicker of the tube. Still we were glad of the
lazy diversion and the excuse not to talk. One of the hundred things we'd agreed not to mention was how I planned

to get to Juniper. I had a dozen friends with cars, and buses were thick on the roads.

But three nights before my departure, Mother brought me a dish of lemon ice cream and said "I apply for the chauffeuring job."

I drew an honest blank.

"To drive you to camp. I'd enjoy that if you would."

I knew she was struggling for nonchalance, but her face couldn't have looked anymore like a wound if I'd struck her a blow. I asked if she could take the time off.

She said "If we left Saturday morning, I could be back by dark Sunday. I've already asked for Saturday off. I'm still the best driver you know."

The last claim was true and still is. She drove the way Fred Astaire danced, as if her fingers were putting out green leaves with no pain or work. I sat there spooning cream, trying to deny what I entirely understood. This woman had manufactured me after all. I'd lived inside her body nine months. I saw and felt every atom of pride it cost her to ask that. I'd all but bought a bus ticket that day, but I said "I'd be honored."

NOW IT'S A BRISK TWO HOURS ON THE INTERSTATE, BUT THEN Asheville was a hard uphill four hours. The whole way we both held in. There'd be long stretches of silence. And if either one of us spoke, it was mostly a reference to sights on the roadside. Thirty years ago once you were in the mountains, there were numerous craftsmen's displays by the road. You could see fine baskets and hooked rugs, salt-glazed crocks and churns of the good old kind, and chenille bedspreads in poisonous chemical colors. Peacocks strutting, dawn in the Smokies, the whole Last Supper down to the spilled salt.

We stopped at several of those. And at the last one, I un-thinkingly bought a three-by-five cornucopia hooked rug for the vestibule at home. The pattern was primitive but the colors were worthy of a Persian weaver. And that did it.

Mother was not a hair-trigger weeper, so there were no tears. But the silence right after I bought the rug was deeper than before. And at last with Asheville in sight, she said "Bridge, let me say it now and don't stop me. You buying that rug was the most help anybody's given me yet."

Again my lifelong blood share in the depths of this woman's mind rescued me. She stopped there, thank God. But I suddenly knew the truth she'd beat me to. Her house was my home; in the face of my marriage a few· years off, it would be my home till the day she died. One of the few things I'll say for myself here is this, I had the guts then to spell it out for her and say she was right.

JUNIPER WAS FORTY-FIVE MINUTES PAST ASHEVILLE IN thick green country. You turned off the paved road and fol-lowed a narrowing dirt trail up through small cedars and junipers, then on till the normal trees were shrubs beside the huge waisted two-hundred-foot hemlocks. And then you broke out of dark into sunlight—the camp itself. It covered the equivalent of a long city block with the Jenkins home, the dining hall and the lodge. Then scattered up the hill were the crafts and Indian lore cabin, some other log build-ings, a field for archery and tetherball and all other sports. Then climbing steeply for two hundred yards was the wide horseshoe of residential cabins and bathhouses.

Mother and I had a prior understanding, a lot like the ones adolescents force on their parents. She was going to drop me off at the lodge. We'd say our goodbye and she'd

drive off, with no looking around, no introductions. Childish as it was, it turned out to be a good idea. I was almost
the last counselor to arrive; and dungareed young men were
loping all around us—they weren't called Levi's or jeans for
years to come. A few of the urban types even had new axes,
well on their way to woodsmanship.

I'D BEEN AN EAGLE SCOUT, WITH PALMS. SO I DIDN'T HAVE
that much to learn about chopping and sawing, axe sharp-
ening, fire building and such open-fire delicacies as dough
on a stick and pork and beans, heated. The classes were
conducted on a broad rock shelf near the top of the mountain to the north of Juniper. On Monday it too would be the
site of a camp, an elite survivalist outfit for boys from fifteen to eighteen. The empty campground consisted of little
more than a clutch of ramshackle tree houses from the previous year. The first task for this year's boys would be the
erasure of last year's work and the building of their own tree
houses. They called it Tsali after a hero of the nearby Cherokees, and a good deal of the curriculum involved an effort
to recover Indian skills that our great-grandfathers had lied,
cheated, stolen and killed to eradicate.

As I said, I marked time through the woodlore classes,
thinking such unproductive thoughts. But after we'd eaten the
good beans, bacon and biscuits, Chief Jenkins stood in the
midst of our circle, closer to the fire than I could have managed. With his unpredictable but always wooden gestures, he
gave us an orientation speech that was just a warmer version
of his Winston talk. I've mentioned that he shone among others of his kind. It was on two scores. He had no fleshly designs
on his staff, and he burned the hottest brand of spiritual gasoline I'd ever seen. But that first night I understood something

I'd missed before. Half of Chief's intensity and power came from his brevity and his boxy gestures.

He might be outrageous in his vision of excellence, but he was never boring. His weird little jerks of arm or head proved he meant all he claimed. And no hot-gospel liar could have raised a dime with a body that awkward. But the blue eyes worked even better by firelight. And he ended with something like "*Think about this*, my young friends tonight. Go lie on your cots in the black mountain dark and think this over before you rest. You've agreed to take on, for ten whole weeks, the healthy future of numerous souls. Never once doubt it—these loud wild bodies, these knock-about boys that will try to craze you with pranks and noise are nothing less than souls from God *that you must tend* and send forth from Juniper, better than they came, on the high road to manhood. Think. Please *think*." Generally Chief seemed to quit, not finish, any speech he gave, so he sat down then. The head counselor took over—Sam Baker, another sane enthusiast. During the school year Sam taught at a nearby boys' school; and his slightest move revealed his foundry, which was the U.S. Marines. He followed Chief's spiritual generalities with a cool rundown on problems to expect. In declining order they were homesickness, cursing, bedwetting, exhibitionistic masturbation in boys over twelve and constipation. And that was about it for problems apparently. Sam finished by mentioning the camp infirmary, with its nurse. But he issued no special warnings on health, despite the fact that we were barely clinging to the flank of a granite mountain in untamed forest stocked with bears and panthers, bobcats and rattlers.

Then Sam sat down and I could see I was not alone in feeling the powerful wash from his wave. All of us counselors looked at each other and shook our heads. They were entrusting each of us—none of whom was a father or even a husband—with fourteen live human children, seven every five weeks. And this was it for orientation?

Once he sat down Sam did add the word that he'd be underfoot around the clock for on-the-spot advice.

I'd been nursing an inward smile of superiority to all this fervor. But at that point I remember it dawned on me, *They're taking me seriously.* That was a raw experience for me, the standard sheltered child of my time and place. Wasn't my generation the first that middle-class America decided to keep in childhood well beyond the age of twenty? Till that night anyhow no one else but my dying father had turned to me and said *You're it.* It thrilled me more than not.

And the final hour only tuned me higher. We didn't actually toast marshmallows, but we sat in a loose circle around the big fire. Sam asked us to introduce ourselves, so we went around the circle and heard each man. The oldest was Roger the swimming counselor, and he was not yet twenty-five. Most of us were sophomore or junior students at small colleges in the Carolinas. Some were bound for the service; Korea was still in arms and hungry for every boy it could get. Two were engaged to be married, one at the end of these ten weeks and the other at Thanksgiving. We were children who thought you should streak out of childhood as fast as you could, and we were the last such American generation.

The immediately remarkable person was Kevin Hawser. With one year to go at Yale, and in a tight race to graduate first in his class, Kevin was the Robert Redford among us. He was six foot three—built strongly with a frank open face.

He was also an expert pianist in all brands of music and a jaw-dropping magician. Not that he spoke that self-servingly on the first night. Those were facts that transpired in the course of the summer. But there at the campfire, I saw that Kev was likely to be my nearest friend.

I told them I was Bridge Boatner from Winston-Salem, that I had a year left at the University of North Carolina in Chapel Hill and that then I was hoping to get a Fulbright and study art in Europe, preferably France or Italy. Somebody asked if I wasn't worried about the draft? I was able to say truthfully that, as the only son of a widowed mother, I was exempt.

Several sang out "Luck-y!" and laughed. Since that was what I'd secretly felt since we knew Father was dying, I was still touchy about it.

But Chief said "A thoroughly merciful provision," and attention passed to the man beside me.

After that Chief rose a last time. Again he thanked us; again in general terms he reminded us of our high privilege and duty. And then he added a revelation. "Up there, high over Tsali on that ledge, is the well of Juniper's sacred strength. It's an Indian prayer circle scraped in the ground, packed by dozens of grown men's feet and ringed with dozens of crude sticks. Each stick is the sign of one man's pilgrimage. It is my fondest hope that, whatever your denomination, each of you will find your own way there before summer ends and pledge your life to the sacrificial service of all mankind. Some of you may think it looks a little high. Some may even think the idea is childish. It's not the most accessible spot—that was intentional. But eat this plentiful simple food, drink this spring water, firm your limbs in weeks of service; and you'll find the climb seems far more possible. It's not a secret we share with campers. That is vital for you to remember. They're not yet strong enough in limb or spirit. But before ten weeks has finished here, each one of you will have the limbs to do it. The only question will concern your *spirit*. Will you need to and want to? The place is waiting.'' He drilled us a final blast from the eyes—Chief invented the laser years early—and sat back down.

Then Uncle Mike Dorfman, a genuinely skilled musician and anthropologist, led us in singing old camp songs. Any of the millions of Americans who are veterans of the camps of the 1940s and '50s are likely to join me in saying that very few later experiences ever match the shivering joy that can well up at such a time, in such a circle. Maybe there was a whiff of Hitler Youth muscularity in the tradition, though weak and awkward boys were not reviled. But the fact remains that, at the right time and in the right place, campfire singing equaled Handel for laughing grandeur against the night—''Tell Me Why the Ivy Twines,'' ''Cocaine Bill and His Wifey Sue'' and the endless and mystical ''Green Grow the Rushes.''

At the very last Mike taught us the Indian words and melody for a prayer to the Great Spirit. I've never since attempted to look it up and discover which language it's in or whether the chromatic melody is authentic or was harmonized for paleface ears. But this much is in my memory still, in crude phonetic spelling—

Wakonda day do, wap-a-deen aton-hay. (Repeat)

All I remember is, Wakonda is the Great Spirit; and the prayer asks for blessing. But there in the cold thin air under starlight, with a dying fire and a band of brothers, it shivered *my* timbers the first time around, and we sang it twice. Then everybody rose for the trip down to bed.

More than one of us paused and tried to make out the prayer circle in darkness. I thought I could see the line of a crag. Whatever, I knew that, since I was burdened with a lifelong stock of awe, I'd climb to that circle and pledge my father the rest of the life denied to his brave weak body. Or pledge it to God, one or the other. Back then to be sure, I was thinking with some of Chief's wide-eyed fever, though for my generation I was no fuming zealot.

MY BED WAS AN UPPER, JUST INSIDE THE DOOR OF CABIN 16. It consisted of a piece of canvas stretched between two boards. There were mattress pads piled on the bunk below me, but a quick inspection by lantern light showed concentric stains from decades back. So until I could sun them, I decided to sleep on the bare canvas, however cold. The mountain nights could freeze, even in June. And with no more preparation, I vaulted up fully dressed with a single army blanket and listened to the night. There was not the usual summer din of frogs, cicadas and the whine of bats. Instead there was silence of such a brown depth as to make me feel a warning twinge of the all but lethal sickness I suffered the one time I was a camper. I longed for home.

For years I'd been convinced that I'd outgrown the problem. Children of the Depression and Second War years seldom went far from home. If your parents had the money, they didn't have the gas or vice versa. So at age eleven my first camp experience ambushed me. After the first few days of novelty, I began to watch this great sink hole open in my heart and spread. By the end of the first week, I couldn't even remember how my parents looked, much less sounded. I strongly suspected they wouldn't show up to get me at the end of the month. This taste of freedom I'd been tricked into giving them would have turned the tide. Why would they want me back in their midst?

By the fourth and last week, I was so hungry for their faces that I'd have eaten a picture of them if you'd brought me one. When the month ended and they reappeared smiling—and at the farewell banquet, I won a Best Boy shield, one of seven—I realized with amazement that I'd managed to conceal my misery. But if I look back and weigh the terrors of a lifetime, I come across very few times more painful than those weeks of wanting my home as the desert wants rain.

But that was ten years behind me. I was grown. I'd traveled meanwhile and lived alone through six semesters of college. So what was this ambush, at Juniper tonight? It came anyhow as a need for the place—the actual two-story, cool frame house with my hermit's cave high up in the back. I saw no visions of Father's or Mother's faces. I heard no keening cries, but I felt a famished craving—*Take me back.* I'd never reneged on a promise as big as I'd made to Chief, but God knew how I would last ten weeks in this ludicrous job.

I recalled I hadn't prayed. College religion courses, with their demonstrations of what a grab bag the poor old Bible is, had pushed my childish faith to the edge of agnosticism. And my prayers by then were mainly a list of the names I loved. Luckily my two parental families were huge. So with selections from their names and with the addition of friends my age, I had another fifteen minutes of meditation. As they mostly did, the names soon turned into handholds on life.

They were people who watched me with expectation and whom I hoped to amaze. Just turning their names back and forth in my mind, like smooth creek stones, was a kind of prayer.

Then the idea of prayer led on into planning my prayer circle climb and trying to see designs for my stick. I was already old enough to know when an idea was meant for me; and this plainly was, a beautiful place with a noble purpose. Chief had also mentioned prayer sticks as craft possibilities, another big attraction. I knew at once that I'd wait till the last day, far down in August. Not till then would I know how to thank the Spirit and what to ask next.

I even thought that my prayer stick might have a carved skull on the top—King Death. I'd stood three feet away, six months ago, and watched Father die. I was the only young man I knew who'd actually seen a human death, in a room with normal furniture, as real as a sneeze. So my thoughts were as bone-strewn as any slaughterhouse. But they wore me out in a few more minutes. In the frigid black I pulled my one blanket tighter around me and fell on sleep like a safety net.

THE NEXT MORNING WAS SUNDAY, SO WE PUT ON OUR white shirts and trousers. Then after breakfast we climbed to yet another prominence. This one was a high field with tall oaks, which for some reason was called the Pasture. And there we took seats to hear the first of Chief's sermons. Strictly speaking it was about the fourth sermon I'd heard from Chief. If he said "You're looking well today," it sounded sermonical, like an elegy on all your wasted days. And his favorite gesture was the classic pulpit chop, right-hand axe on lefthand stump. His text was the parable of the

Prodigal Son from the gospel of Luke, and he meant to prepare us to cherish even the most troublesome boy in our care. For all his up-and-at-em vigor, Chief always included the weak and needy boy. You couldn't find a boy he'd spurn or despise.

I admired that in him, but the main thing I heard that Sunday morning was a confirmation of my resolve from the night before. At the end of the parable, when the bereaved father embraces his lost son, I fought back tears and swore to have a sizable life.

One of the last things my father said to me was "Anybody on Earth can be *common*, son." In the idiom of his time, the word *common* was harsher by far than *shit* is now. *Common* meant absolutely *natural*, people who settled for being themselves, with their shirttails out. He'd been balked in his own hopes to practice law. I must not be balked, whatever my dream. Somehow he'd spared me the weight of substitute success. He never asked me to excel because he hadn't. But the meaning hung there before me from the start. And oh, no starved white-trash hound was ever hungrier for rabbit than I was for greatness in the eyes of Heaven and Earth.

If you remember the bottomless, and topless, innocence of the 1950s, you'll find it easier to believe me when I say that—alongside a healthy appetite for fun, sex, tennis, swimming and most kinds of music—I was a starved consumer of the highest art. My room at college was a tabernacle to the Greeks, Michelangelo, Vermeer, Picasso, Winslow Homer, Handel, Wagner, Keats, Hemingway and T. S. Eliot. From an Italian trip a teacher had brought me five or six of the uncanny Alinari reproductions of Michelangelo's most ethereal drawings. So over my bed hung such high-water marks as "Archers Shooting at a Herm," "The Fall of Phaeton," a study of the Last Judgment and so on.

On a New York trip, for fifty dollars I'd purchased a fragment of a Greek girl. It was just a lopped-off torso but it glowed. My mellow RCA phonograph was backed by a respectable library of classical and jazz and blues album. And the low bookcase held the cream of a library I'd accumulated since childhood. There were poems, novels, the lives of great artists and every Phaidon art book I could find. I'd have killed for copies of the prewar Phaidons I couldn't find—Giorgione, Titian and El Greco.

I not only owned them, I used them all. Years before Father suffered and died, I combined their exalted visions of human potential with my own boyhood fantasies about Young Jesus, the one who astounded the scholars in the Temple. And I came up with high ambitions. Now with the memories of Father and his final challenge not to be common, the goal shone brighter. It spun ever faster and it seemed to draw near. I wanted to earn, I wanted truly to deserve, the permanent thanks of mankind. I wanted my good-sounding name to last. It was not impossible. A few dozen men had actually done it, a few strong women. Therefore I could.

I'm painfully aware how crazy that sounds. Even at the time, I suspected I was all but certifiable. Before I reached Juniper though, I'd confided to no one. Despite the ecstatic imagery of my plan, the practical means were within the reach of hope. I would paint, or make with whatever tools, pictures of the world that compelled belief. And belief not only in the reality of the world and its worthiness for contemplation and honor but a whole lot more. I wanted my pictures to inculcate, in secret of course, a trust in the hand that waits behind this brute noble Earth to lead us out and elsewhere.

I meant, in a word, to be a great artist and was far more certain than any of my overimpressed kin and friends of what a long distance lay between me and the goal. And still does, half a normal lifespan later. I mentioned calling myself agnostic. It didn't rule out my firm conviction that nature is *made*. And it gives fairly unmistakable signs of being made by a single force that somehow includes everything. Everything we think of as beautiful and ugly, all good, all evil and a great deal more than we can imagine. I already had twenty-one years of evidence. I planned to get more, with my own two eyes. I mean, if you've never seen a watch or a clock in your life but discover a fine Swiss watch in working order on your walk today, will you just assume it's a natural object—the product of eons of chemical accidents? If so, proceed to the nearest brain-scan machine. You are almost surely in terrible shape.

All of that swam only just below the surface as I sat with the other counselors, heard Chief out and sang "A Mighty Fortress" to Mike Dorfman's pitch. On the amble downhill to lunch, two of the second-timers stage-whispered their boredom with the steadily rising piety level. We laughed them on into perfect imitations of Chief's puppet walk, all lurching knees and elbows. We hadn't noticed but he was just behind us. He saw the mocking and responded with a chuckle that relieved us at least but was more like the usual human response to gastric distress.

That released me. I'd been reared in a household founded on laughter. If a thing couldn't be laughed at, it either hadn't happened or was pitiful. I realized that nobody had laughed yet at Juniper—not in my hearing, certainly not in Chief's, not a belly laugh deep enough to ventilate the mind. So I joined in the general relief and was still laughing ten minutes later when the soup came round.

Finally Kevin Hawser said "It's just *life*, Bridge." Then he sang " 'Don't take it serious; it's too mysterious.' "

I didn't know it was from an old song, but it sounded true enough to calm me down.

Then we changed into work clothes and spent the rest of Sunday, on into the night, getting the cabins and the other buildings ready for Monday's fabled onslaught of boys.

THE BOYS PRETTY WELL TOOK CARE OF THEMSELVES. PARents were the work. From what I gathered in their applications, six of my seven boys were first-timers here. That meant six chances for distraught mothers and pining boys. And since all my boys were in the middle age group, ten to twelve, I also anticipated the problems of that painful fulcrum between frank childhood and the musky outskirts of puberty. There'd be the scorn of older boys for younger and the opposite in romantic worship—moon-eyed crushes by the younger boys. By suppertime anyhow I had a full cabin, nobody was dead or in traction yet, and I'd suffered few mamas.

Chief had suggested strenuously that taking money from parents for favors was an unworthy idea. And one father tried it, in appropriate whispers. His son was a bedwetter, despite the application's urging that such boys might feel uncomfortable. Would I conspire with the child to conceal any mishaps from the others? When I told him I'd survived the same heartache myself and would do my best, his eyes filled; and he pressed a wadded fifty into my palm. He was one of the bigger Carolina textile magnates—I'd known his name in the paper for years—and from the look of relief on his face, I saw that if I'd known of a cure for belated bed-wetting, I could have named my fee. As it was, fifty dollars back then was serious money. But entirely against my will, I returned it.

One mother presented a handsome King James New Testament, bound in olive wood from the Holy Land, with the words of Jesus in red ink. She said she'd just feel better knowing that the cabin had a Bible but that in August I should take it home with me. When I thanked her she also whispered that she didn't want her Teddy to hear the Bible read in any translation but the "Saint James." There'd been hot grass-roots objections to the recent publication of the Revised Standard Version, which cast some shadow on the Virgin Mary's virginity. I told her Teddy would be safe from such harm. And after that the other boys and parents seemed normal. There were several damp good-byes—five weeks apart!—but by suppertime we were all campers banded together, and the forging of a temporary family was underway.

TO MY GENUINE PLEASURE IT WENT SMOOTHLY, RIGHT along. As we lay in the dark that first night, telling our names and backgrounds aloud, a boy said straightforwardly that his mother had died last November and that he wasn't "as strong as I want to be yet." He said it out slowly, taking each word like a stepping-stone through rapid water. So I could tell that he knew his audience and still had the nerve to say it. I'm proud to record that no one snickered or ever used it against him, and he ended as one of the popular boys.

One boy from High Point was clearly in the early stages

of hormonal tumult and said so, something like "I'm turning into a grownup faster than I planned to, but so far it's
right much fun to watch."

The bedwetter went straight to the brink of confession.
"My father says I've got some habits that camp will help,
which is why I came. I hope y'all will help me." That
plea, in its abject dignity, was as brave as it was reckless.
And again I'm glad to say that it got him a smooth five
weeks with the others.

The rest had nothing peculiar to add.

So I finished off by telling them about my father's death
early last winter and of my hope to lay that behind me
during ten weeks of mountain air, sunlight, fun with them
and a lot of good work. It wasn't quite out of my mouth
before I thought that was too scary for them, this first night
anyhow. And for half a minute, they all were so quiet I
thought they'd gone to sleep or were sobbing or chewing
their pillows.

But then the boy who'd lost his mother said "Why do you
want your daddy behind you? I want Mother back in front
of me."

I told him gently that was probably because he was eleven
and I was twenty-one, the kind of damned-fool thing you
say at twenty-one.

He said "I won't be twenty-one then. I liked to watch
her. Her hair was the best-smelling stuff I know."

Before I could muster a second wise answer, a volumi-
nous fart tore the cold like a lit powder trail—the loudest
I'd heard. A faceless voice said "How's that for good smell-
ing?" Then monkey-house laughter, boys hopping out of
bunks accusing one another and fanning their outraged de-
lighted noses. The boy with the dead mother led the glee.

I silently reminded my upstaged self that body wind in its two main forms, belches and farts, is half the foundation of boyish humor. I rightly suspected I'd hardly begun to experience their virtuosity in ways to smuggle farts like anarchist bombs into the highest and most sacred scenes of camp life. In fact the rest of the summer was, from one angle anyhow, a crash training course in ballistic wind tactics. Their supreme goal turned out to be a feat called the "S.B.D.," a *silent but deadly* fart—the anonymous invisible outrage that left a room gasping. If no one guessed the culprit within thirty seconds, he got to cry "S.B.D.!" in triumph and could hit us all, one good hard punch.

Finally that first night I corralled them back down, called for the customary Lord's Prayer and tumbled on sleep as easily as they.

AN ORDERLY REPORT ON THAT FIRST FIVE WEEKS WOULD raise a number of laughs and more than one lump in the throat, but the jokes and poignancy of Camp Juniper in June and early July 1954 were thoroughly typical of the American camp life that has since been the subject of numerous comic songs, movies and TV series. Only one of the boys, the son of the camp's dietitian and a four-year veteran of Juniper, posed an early problem—mainly verbal defiance and an effort to demoralize the cabin with jokes about every adult in sight. When I discovered that his parents were recently divorced, which was a rarity then in the South, I stumbled on a benign paternal tack. I told him that, as a new counselor, I needed his advice. From that moment on I'd confide my puzzlement at this or that. He'd set me straight as an old Dutch uncle and from then on was a mainly stalwart help.

The bedwetter never confided an accident. The orphan had a few desolate moments—one morning, when he and I were alone in the cabin, out of the absolute blue he told me he didn't believe in Heaven—but he never shed a tear that I got to see. And the others pitched in with mostly unfailing good humor. There were normal frictions, bruised feelings and one or two black eyes. But to my knowledge there was none of the meanness normal in childhood. The best I can say about them is that they occasionally made me regret being an only child and missing such robust company.

We all slept in the same open space, and we dressed and undressed in full view of one another. We ate our meals at the same table, washed in the same bathhouse. And once a week we went on a cabin supper together. That consisted of maybe a three-mile hike, followed by a campfire-cooked meal, ghost stories, songs and a night on the ground. So my claim of close knowledge is probably safe. The only substantial time they spent out of my sight was during the morning and afternoon classes. Then they were off taking archery, art, diving, horseback riding, magic, Indian lore, pottery, swimming and woodcraft. And there they were watched by other counselors. As summers go then—and boys—it was an unblemished start.

I TAUGHT DRAWING AND WATERCOLOR PAINTING FIVE mornings a week. And I single-handedly wrote, typed, mimeographed and stapled *The Thunderbird* in the afternoons. The paper was easy and boring but of evident importance to Chief. He'd told me in Winston how, once a year, he sent a complete set of papers to the Asheville Library, where they were carefully preserved "for after times." And I realized that, such as it was, Chief saw *The*

Thunderbird as history. Somewhere a hundred years from now, we'd all be dead—and all these boys and their grandchildren—but a set of mimeographed weekly papers would be the surviving record of his work and his life's devotion. Not to mention its revelations that Bill Grimsley had won the intermediate horseshoe tournament, David Holt had plaited a yard-long key chain or that Mrs. Chief was safely back from a visit to her bedridden sister in Aurelian Springs.

Still Chief paid frequent visits to my office in the lodge. He said he only meant to encourage me, and he'd often deliver the latest of his brief but clarion editorials. But I understood he was also checking the health of the trust he'd placed in me. Was I thinning out, in mind or soul, towards the kind of break that often delays after a personal crisis but strikes unexpected one calm afternoon? Was my dead father riding me still? I'll grant that Chief managed his checks with a pawky grace. He'd always ask for news of my mother, or he'd say he noticed how proud the boys in my art class looked. *Proud* was very high praise from Chief, but beneath it I also heard his fear. And I tried to let him see I was safe.

My other main work was the art class. At the first interview Chief had spoken of my offering a "serious" class. I decided it was better not to probe the meaning of that—unless he volunteered advice, which he never did. So when I planned the activities, I leaned heavily on the traditional methods that I'd learned privately from an excellent woman in Winston and was repeating now in college. Plus a few innovations from my reading in the lives of painters, in Michelangelo's letters, Delacroix's diary and the notebooks of Gauguin and Leonardo.

Hard as I tried though, my Juniper classes were steadily but not surprisingly disappointing. Public schools then had

no funds at all for teaching art. After an early run at fin-
gerpainting with garish mud, and at drawing with broken
and peeled crayons, we were bustled on to the meat of life.
That was math, grammar and writing the business letter.
So none of the campers had really studied art before meeting me. And to be honest, in the first session I felt lucky
not to have a gifted pupil. I thought he would have drained
my energy and stood between me and my own work. I
hadn't yet experienced the teacher's best reward. If you're
lucky, that comes on the unpredictable day when the years
of classroom rock-crushing suddenly begin to feed into your
own work. You find that you understand human life, and
you still want to paint it.

Meanwhile twice a week I set up still lifes or led the boys
to interesting views, plants or rock formations in the middle
distance, and turned them loose. I never left though till I'd
given some version of the only useful advice I'd heard in
my own training—*Look, really look. The boundary lines of
the natural world are tracing a lot more complicated route
than you think at first. Watch the line of your leg, the trunk
of that tree, the split in your face through which you feed.*
Or to put it quicker, *Things don't often look the way you
think they do. Pay them the simple honor of watching their
lines and shadows till they tell you their secrets. Those are
the codes of life and of life's own draftsmen.*

Was that any quicker? Maybe I can no longer recover the
naive advice I gave that summer. A dredge of my memory
finds what I've written above. And since it has a dim but
true ring still, then I could be recalling correctly. It's the
implied and beatific "wisdom" that convinces me. Who but
a very young and privileged white American, unaccustomed

to hearing a discouraging word, would claim that much in public and for pay?

WHATEVER I SAID, HOWEVER I BEGGED, THEIR COPIES OF everything were dogged and lifeless and scared. Like most people they were helpless to copy appearances. Their images were either small and cramped as microbes or big as pumpkins. There'd be tiny boiled-down mountains or a gaseous wallowing bowl of peaches on the verge of crowding people off the planet. I'd patrol their easels and drawing boards, exhorting attention, pleading for scale. Let the peach on paper be the realer peach, the one you'd rather have.

I was behind on my reading of contemporary fiction and poetry. So I didn't know that, at that moment in San Francisco and New York, Gary Snyder and Jack Kerouac·were urging the same. *Transcribe the world!* They thought of their method as Buddhist. I thought of mine as Christian, but I kept that to myself.

Hadn't Jesus gone to great lengths, in numbers of parables, to teach just that? Only the endlessly watchful life is worth living and will be rewarded. *What I say to you, I say to all—watch!* And by *watchful* he didn't mean condemning or fearful but attentive. You watch your particular set of external objects because you love, or at least respect, them on faith. And because you watch them, you train that respect to know them better. Then you go on watching with an even deeper, though maybe more painful, devotion.

WAS I BADLY OFF COURSE, FOR MY TIME AND PLACE? WHO isn't, in his or her early twenties? They're an even more self-intoxicated age than adolescence. If I was at fault, and most times I think I was, then my mistake lay in operating on such a highfalutin base with creatures as impressionable as boys. Sometimes still I defend myself by saying that not a soul in camp, in either session, knew the contents of my mind. They had only my acts to watch and my words to hear. And those were straightforward performances of daily duty, salted with what I hoped was enough wit for freshness and the prevention of boredom.

Whatever light my thinking cast as a torch for my own life and work, I kept it a secret dynamo humming at the center of my mind. For me it lit every sketch I drew, every roll call, every tick hunt. On Sunday mornings after Saturday jamborees, we checked each boy for the all too common tick. Ticks could give you Rocky Mountain spotted fever, and most boy's scalps were studded with ticks after any short hike, but again nobody came down with anything worse than the sniffles. Even my own two sons, when they hit adolescence twenty-five years later—they barely glanced up from their own self-regard to hear my stream of tactful suggestions. For all they knew, or cared apparently, I might just be a money-secreting fungus on the ground at their feet. More lately here though, things have improved.

But in the 1950s if a lot of my guidance came from the life of Jesus, then was I a Christian? I still believed that the man Jesus was a good deal more than a man and had died in some entirely mysterious way as a blood sacrifice for you and me. So my big problem was not with him but with the outfits that called themselves "his" church. When I read in Carl Jung that religion was a way to avoid having religious experiences, I heard my own mind. It still impresses me no little that, in the whole New Testament, Jesus goes to church—synagogue—not more than twice by my count, and each time it gets him in serious trouble.

I've mentioned being raised a Presbyterian, and I'd sat through Sunday school and several hundred sermons in my childhood and teens. And in college I'd already taken more than the one required Bible course, but back at age nineteen the church and I had agreed to separate. I thought church religion was good for who it was good for, and that I was no good for it or it for me. That meant, by the time I was in college, I'd basically become an agnostic mystic, if that sounds vague enough. I don't mean a man who sits out naked and stares at the sun till his eyeballs boil. Or a self-flagellator whose tortured flesh is now and then rewarded with visions of God as an oiled sexy lover.

I just mean a person who feels inspired to conduct his own relations with the mainline energy behind creation. What's agnostic is that I'm sure the mainline circuit is something far too complicated for me, or any other creature, to know entirely—much less map out for future control. In light of what's coming later here, I need to say that none of this means that I can't get roused at the right time and place to some fairly hot feelings and acts. I can.

I mean I've got down on my knees and kissed the spot in Jerusalem where Jesus' dead body almost certainly lay till it came to life, and I feel no shame in saying as much. Places get holy, some rare few places; and you want to know what's what and when to bow. After the real-estate agents have had their century of freedom in America, there's little enough left where you can even see dirt, much less the god in it. So you've got to keep looking. You can't just prostrate yourself at every crossroads tomb of a president or other licensed killer. That's idol worship and is also indecent.

* * *

IF YOU'RE YOUNG AND MALE, WORKING LONG DAYS AND eating great helpings of farm-fresh food in mountain air with unlimited butter, milk, cheese and ice cream, then your main problem with decency is going to be sex. Now well on in my sixth decade—age fifty-four—and hardly out of the running, I can recall the unquenchable erotic fury of those years with awe and frank pride. The awe comes from looking back and seeing my long slender body seized at the waist, in the vast and thoroughly capable jaws of Eros, and *shook*. In my case serious shaking began in the sixth grade and continued, with no more than breathers for food and laundry, till my late forties when the jaws seemed a little less fierce than before, though by no means weak.

Young people in the 1960s announced that they'd discovered free sex. They proceeded to give each other fleas and to bore the rest of us speechless right on till now when the immense and incalculable horror of AIDS promises to alter mankind's sexuality and our cell-by-cell feeling for the loveliness of human flesh more profoundly than anything else in history, syphilis included. People after all occasionally recovered from syphilis or endured mild cases, even before treatments were discovered and the spirochete had picked off Beethoven, Schubert, Baudelaire, Flaubert, Verlaine and Gauguin just to start the roll.

But we in the 1950s were supremely lucky, I still think, in maturing at a time when sex was not in the glare of public lights. You could sleep with your girlfriend or sister or a whore or the boy next door or for that matter with your parents. And there wouldn't be a pollster, a welfare worker or a representative of CBS News standing by the bed waiting for the heaves to subside so he could ask you to rate your experience for sensory reward and moral value.

There were a lot of virgins among us, of all ages and genders. There were also a lot of thoroughly industrious indulgers, male and female. They were recognizable only by a faint though enviable smile and a refusal to talk or above all to brag. Between the extremes lay the frustrated millions who claimed to be in mortal need but who were secretly relieved to have a few more years of passive seasoning in the cave of adolescence before rushing onto the drenched and floodlit field of combat. Whichever, if you needed a little pornography to help you in your anatomy lessons and to buff your imagination, it could always be found cheap at the tobacconist's or on grade-school playgrounds. Recall those late-lamented and elegantly drawn funny books where Sandy was boarding an eager Orphan Annie, or Popeye in full spinach frenzy was transporting Olive to the heights of bliss?

If you fell into the majority of American male youth, you went to your room and joined the silent majority of self-servers, again and again and again. Unfortunately sexual surveys had not yet permeated us guilt-crazed youngsters with the news that we *were* the overwhelming majority. So we labored alone—shamefully producing, casting and running our own mental movies for an audience consisting, safely but sadly, of our lone selves.

I'll add only that, in line with my policy of decency where possible, I adopted a rule for my sexual fantasies. I could not cast any real girl or woman in my head movies unless she'd given me permission to do so. Permission could be given in two ways. Either she had already appeared in real movies and thus offered herself for fantasy work or she, in person, had permitted me sufficient liberties. This rule, strict as it was, still left me Rita Hayworth, Jane Russell and Marilyn Monroe, not to mention a few good sports on my block and at school.

To be brief I arrived at Juniper as a thoroughly debauched yet technical virgin. I had not quite had intercourse but almost, a few dozen times. I'd had no regular sweetheart since my four-year high-school girlfriend left me for the quarterback, literally. At college I'd gone out with several of the blazingly intelligent and witty girls of that era, the female inhabitants of early Roth and Updike stories. One in particular—a tall brunette from Lyme, Connecticut—was my principle resource.

She finished my education in female parts. And we laughed our way through it, together or in distended letters when we were separated, as now. By mail we'd make flat-out full love. But in real life at the end of our stupendously successful games, she would always find my dilated eyes and say sadly "We aren't meant to do this forever, you know?" The fact that she always stopped us from doing it *all*—and the further fact that our hair and eyes were duplicates of one another and that people often mistook us for siblings—gives the memory of us a weird lovely spin, even today. Bad as it hurt, I guess she was right. We weren't meant to do it.

So understand that I got to Juniper—wondering if I was meant to, ever, go all the way? And while I plan to avoid boring insistence on the matter, anyone hoping to understand this story will need to recall that, all through the summer, I was fired up in that whole territory too and that my one self-administered vent was far from sufficient to cool me safely. The constant and comic sight of prepubescent male bodies served only to remind me that I—a man already past the flood tide of reproductive power but roaring—was

still, practically speaking, as nearly a eunuch as they with
their pitiful tubular hairless frames and trembling blue tad-
pole dicks.

Finding ten minutes alone for self-fulfillment was a near
impossibility. You'd have thought a camp in the midst of
wild forest would be ideal. But I tried locking the *Thunderbird* door only to have Chief insert his pass key and almost
catch me. I hiked up the mountain behind Cabin 16 and
found a secluded mossy niche only to have two of my boys
scramble up noisily, with their new Indian pathfinding skills,
and ask was I safe? My only hope was to wait past their
bedtime, count all their breaths by way of roll call, then
quickly dispatch myself in the freezing black night. It was
sad deprivation for a body young as mine and so eager to
please.

IF I MISSED SEX, I DIDN'T MISS LOVE. MAYBE I'VE BEEN
abnormal in that. But from late childhood, I've got pretty
much all the love I needed in doing my work. I've thought
all along anyhow, and hoped, that my painting absorbs and
focuses and returns to the viewer most of the energy that
normally flows into love. From watching other humans I
have to guess that *love* is a steady longing for the presence
and betterment of one or more other humans. If that's the
case then I have to say now that, with the huge exception
of my two sons, I doubt I've known much human love—not
since leaving the shelter of both my parents. I've understood
sex fairly well, I think. God knows, I've enjoyed its varieties, from the howling barnyard buck-and-buckle to the
mute conjugation of souls in flesh.

And I gave all I had to an early marriage, honestly all.
My wife and the mother of both my sons was and is a

splendid creature. She just had far more to give than I needed. It was mostly good and any other ten sane men on the street would have dropped to their knees and begged to get it, her hundred daily proofs of care. But her steady attention had worried me early; and once we were married, it was soon our torment. I hated to keep refusing her overflow. And for three long years I managed to take it. They were the years that brought sons. Then my whole mind balked. This was way too much, and I began to show it in ways too shameful and small to own up to. We hurt each other through six more years, and then we parted with the sad respect of animals too numb to go on fighting. And of course we shared real thanks and amazement for two sturdy boys, each better than us.

Since then my roaming but fastidious erotic curiosity, with my basic dread of loneliness and the standard need to pass my findings along to a fellow human, has won me several long intimacies, with big gifts and receipts. But they've yet to compel me to want one woman—or Labrador—steadily. And with that limitation I've continued to balk at the final marriage jump, though I've known an irregular sequence of helpmates that ranged from wonderful to sweet-but-awful. Maybe the visible outskirts of age will begin to change that.

ANYHOW AT JUNIPER I WROTE JOURNAL LETTERS TO MY girlfriend and sent her dozens of sketches, more than one of them anatomical, and several finished watercolor landscapes. But the great part of all my various energies went toward painting and my camp routines. In that I wasn't remarkable. All my age mates groaned but bore the deprivations. And when we all gathered most nights in the counselors' hut after lights out, I could easily join their rail-

ing and joking. We'd sort the day's take of camper horrors,
like the boy who tried to circumcise himself with dull scis-
sors or the boy who hadn't had a b.m. in three weeks, then
was delivered of a nine-pound wonder that two boys re-
corded on Polaroid film.

And by then we'd honed our imitations of Chief to perfection and had turned to work on Mrs. Chief, a flawless
Victorian matron with remorselessly even porcelain teeth
and breastworks that might have saved Richmond from
Grant. I could also silently monitor their minds and com-
pare them to my own. We all seemed cheerfully horny—
mean horny waited till the late 1960s—because we'd been
blessed in the same way as most of our contemporaries,
even the two all-but-marrieds. We'd never known regular
mutual sex and were thus not addicted, not truly desperate,
as so many young people plainly are now.

In all it was one of the most likable groups I've ever been
with. Except for the betrothed two and another few who
were going steady, in general they were as loose in the world
as me and as fit to be amazed. The highest ambitions, other
than my own, were held by the man from Yale—Kevin Hawser—and by a would-be lawyer from Wake Forest, Possum
Walters. Otherwise they were politely unexceptional, without ambition but with a vague confidence in working for
their fathers or fathers-in-law or simply throwing themselves
on the mercy of the open market in a floodtime of easy
employment.

To the passing eye, I was very much like them. In only
one visible way was I conspicuous, my drawing and painting. They liked to watch me draw. Any sidewalk incompetent can pull a small crowd in a city. And at Juniper
wherever I sat with my paper and board, I soon had a hud-

dle of whispering watchers. They enjoyed the small thrill I also enjoy when I stumble on a competent public artist. They were spying on what all such spies think of as a splendid magic, "Look, he's making another world." That far, they're right, though it's easier than they think. As I mentioned, you only need to *watch*, then let your hand do exactly what your mind tells it. Eventually one of the bystanders at camp would say "Could you draw me, if you wanted to?" And when I said "If I wanted to," they would laugh and begin to melt away.

LIKE MOST ARTISTS OF ANY DESCRIPTION, I QUICKLY learned how to build my own solitude and concentration, no matter who stood at my shoulder. And that became another wide gulf between me and the world. Most people are all too ready to be jostled. Their work is something they're longing to quit. Wherever I've taught, I've taught that first— the power and joy of oneness, solitude. And for the first three weeks at Juniper, I took my class on walks around the campground, sketching anything and everything.

I'd set one boy to one object. I'd point Chip to a box turtle found in the path; I'd assign Willie to Mrs. Chief's morning glories and Jeff to her old blind collie. Like anywhere else in unroofed nature, the subjects were endless. Take the brown still lake in early morning; guess the mind of this bird fishing in the shallows here, those rocks that mimic every known shape and form, your neighbor's face or the Smoky range in the western distance. That, God knows, was grand as the stride of the young Norse gods into Odin's Valhalla and far more surely immortal in strength. Boys can laugh at anything nearly. But I never heard one of mine laugh at the Smokies.

* * *

IN THE FOURTH WEEK OF THE FIRST SESSION, I GROUNDED
the class with me on the west side of the crafts cabin. And
while they made what they could, in watercolor and pastels,
of the ten thousand values of green and gray between us
and the western horizon, I began the painting I'd been led
to do. No voices in the night, don't worry. But I do mean
led. As I sketched and fiddled in search of a bigger subject,
my mind's eye kept showing me that wide west range. You
might say that I'd have had to be blind to choose anything
else. But there were stunning views to the south—even more
dramatic peaks and crags, including the one with the prayer
circle—and the whole eastward sweep of camp, on up past
my own cabin into taller and thicker trees, was one immense green breast.

What led me to the long horizontal west range was my
growing sense that the line itself was a calligraphed sentence. Those hazy hard peaks on a harder blue sky. It was
some coded combination of meanings that, if ever deci-
phered, would free mankind and forever reward us. I had
few illusions of cracking the code. But as late as that summer, I did believe that if I could transfer the line to canvas
and set all patient watchers to work on the tasks of translation, what grace might I not set loose in the world?

I didn't mean it, not that flatfootedly anyhow. I was
splendidly and crazily fervent, but even that summer I knew
the world better than to tell it my plan to save its soul. All
the same I was as sure then as now that most of the urgent
outstanding secrets of this one universe are strewn here before us. They are barely encoded, in faces and things, and
are patiently waiting for the witness that will solve them.

It will only take a few human beings—light and persistent, saints and artists—who struggle to master the languages that can finally convey such news to the rest of the species. I'll leave it at that, I'm sure you're glad to hear. Few things are more pointless than tries at describing the emotional burden of a visual image to someone who hasn't already seen the image. You can talk half an hour and wind up with a misty little paragraph that sounds like a Kahlil Gibran reject.

In any case I spent more than a week, in my rare hours of personal time, laying the design of that western horizon onto a stretched and primed canvas in meticulous pencil detail. And when the first session ended in mid-July, I was ready to start the stacking up of light and shade in hundreds of almost transparent glazes.

Then with more regret than I'd planned, I helped my first set of boys pack to leave. It was my introduction to one of life's sorrows. In the short but fierce proximities of life—summer camp, painting classes, ocean cruises, army platoons—we only begin seeing our companions in the final few days. And only in those fourth and fifth weeks of the first session at Juniper did I see what I might have had if I'd known how really to *watch* the boys a good while sooner. I'd have had rich lists of their unique brands of small daily heroism, their doggy personal quirks and their thirsty affections. Parting day was a Friday—the mamas and the papas again, beamish this time and with a few more tips, that I shamelessly took.

THE SATURDAY MORNING WAS CLEANUP TIME. EACH COUNselor spread all his cabin's mattress pads out to sun. And it was only then that I realized how successfully my threatened bedwetter had deceived me and his cabin mates. His mattress pad was a swamp of concentric circles of never-dried pee. I hauled it far up into the woods and abandoned it, with a real shudder for the boy who suffered five weeks of cold sodden nights rather than confess.

Sunday was free. I haven't mentioned previous such days. One day a week, once we'd seen our boys through breakfast, we were free till reveille the next morning. Kevin and I usually managed to take the same day off. Since neither one of us had a car, we'd catch a ride into Asheville with some older staff member or we'd hitch.

Now the whole city has been leveled, homogenized and defaced. But back then the pocket-sized town had the irregular charm of a real place. It felt like one whole single thing that had grown in slow response to various needs of people and the land. And in the case of Asheville, the charm was all the greater because of the mountain terrain. A small busy downtown square was overwatched by a ring of still wild mountains, with only the tan stone hulk of the Grove Park Inn staring down. Even the streets were humped here and there by an uncertain grounding.

Kev and I would get there a little after ten. We'd part and do personal errands. Then we'd meet at a particularly generous cafeteria and gorge on what we never got at camp. I remember craving fried eggplant and country-style steak. In the afternoon together we'd hunt through the several old bookstores, then the cafeteria again for supper, a movie, then the trip back to camp. Neither Kevin nor I was a night owl, but it was vital to the notion of a day off that we stay in town till our boys were asleep.

Those few free days have a distinct sweetness in my memory. It comes partly from the fact that, since I'd never had a job before, I'd never known the joy of *not* working.

Mostly though the pleasure comes from remembering the long hours of talk with Kevin. Americans in their early twenties then were still fairly wild to learn their way forward into the world. They'd talk a whole night just to learn some scrap of useful news that they could have found in an almanac in fourteen seconds—say, the manner of death of Catherine the Great, and did it involve her suffocation by an amorous donkey? Kevin and I were in that boat but mainly me. I knew he was further along than me in everything.

Kev's answers to me on a big range of subjects were wide, deep and well-seasoned with wit. They were also land-mined with unexpected questions that kept me constantly on guard. A thoroughly typical case was this. Over strawberry shortcake one day at lunch, I made the strategic error of owning up to a little less than half my ambition for greatness. Kevin heard it straight through with no trace of a smile, and then he asked "What will the world do if you die tonight?" No trace of an edge on his question either. He was just asking for the sake of the news, so he'd know if I croaked.

If I meant then to lay out my wares for Kev, I had to be damned sure they were strong enough to handle and were laid down carefully. You couldn't just tell him that, say, Picasso was greater than Gilbert Stuart. You had to prove it and mostly I couldn't. So breakage was high in any such dialogue. Kev would hold back politely and let you choose the topic. But once you invited him in, he *jumped*. I've said that, because of the recent Depression and war, Americans hadn't traveled much for twenty-five years; and the country was strictly divided into regions. If you'd grown up in Rockford, Illinois, you barely knew anybody from Chicago, much less Winston-Salem.

And Kevin Hawser was the first real Yankee I'd spent time with. I enjoyed the speed and fresh air of our talks, but I also knew what a heavy brake his urban cynicism put on me. I could never let him see the full gleam of my intentions or my plans for reaching them. My sort of dream, in those early days, melted in the presence of laughter. That midsummer Sunday though, Kev set the pace. He asked me the night before if I'd like to join him tomorrow for a "pilgrimage"—the quotation marks were his—to Thomas Wolfe's home. I gladly agreed, though with reservations that will soon appear.

As a native North Carolinian, I knew that the state's most famous artist of any sort was born in Asheville in 1900 and died from tuberculosis of the brain before he was forty. My father, exactly Wolfe's age, had met him briefly in the early twenties. A lot of painters are big readers; so when I began consuming fiction in my teens, Father suggested that I notice his friend Tom Wolfe. In some brand of adolescent truculence, I didn't. Then early in high school, several of my male friends began to echo Father—Thomas Wolfe had apparently solved the mysteries of human longing or had at least captured them in words forever. They confided also that Wolfe wrote a lot about sex, whores and body crabs.

That knocked me off-center, and I rushed out to find him. But the book wasn't in our school library, being thought unfit for innocent eyes. The old dragons at the Public downtown were sleeping for once, so I managed to check out *Look Homeward, Angel*. But even at age sixteen, pitching and tossing in the very flames Wolfe described—youthful sex and vaulting ambition—I thought I knew bad prose when I saw it. And I stopped for good at page fifty.

That didn't keep me from wanting to see his home. Now I hear it's a manicured historical site operated by the state. But in the early fifties, with Wolfe not twenty years dead, it was still owned by members of the family. A rambling white barn of no architectural distinction, it had till fairly recently been a busy boardinghouse run by Wolfe's feisty mother right through his childhood, youth, fame and death.

The front door was open. We knocked on the screen and were met by a pretty young woman with a snotty baby on her hip. We asked if this really was the Wolfe house. She nodded yes, said it cost a quarter and took our money. Then she stepped aside and let us in. Her voice had the high blackboard-scraping harshness of the born mountaineer, but then her prematurely exhausted face broke into a quick smile that I'd still give a lot to paint. It was as good an emblem as I've ever seen for hanging on when the sky's against you.

But she didn't look any the worse for wear. To me, she wore whatever pain she'd borne like an invitation to take one short step and save her life, hers and the smiling girl-baby's she held.

She said "I'm right busy, with the baby and whatnot. And since I ain't been here but a week, I don't know much nohow. So if y'all want to look around, make yourself at home. Just try not to touch things more than you have to. They're precious and all."

We pretty much made ourselves at home. It hadn't dawned on me to wonder what no-nonsense Kevin was seeking here at this font of wind. But it was soon clear that he'd come along in hopes of a postcard to send a professor friend and Wolfe fan. Kev had at least read *Look Home-ward, Angel*; but he kept most of his knowledge to himself as always. Since I couldn't say what had happened in the many rooms of the dim upper warrens, it was pretty much a musty old boardinghouse to me. But there were little hand-lettered cards, saying "Tom's Boyhood Room," "Tom's Boyhood Shakespeare" by a thick black book or "Brother Ben's Deathbed." And even Kevin, an English major, seemed muffled so I stayed respectful. I had to admit to myself that it did have a certain pregnant air, as if a big artist hadn't yet been born but was going to be, here and soon. I used the word *artist* a lot in those days. I thought it would help me grow. But my only clear memory of the house itself is of a huge black pay-phone by the door in a back hallway.

It was the old kind that had so many different comforting odors—one for the metal of the chassis, one for the heavy Bakelite handset, one for the breathed-on mouthpiece, an-other for the thick stiff cord. And it had names and phone numbers still gouged in the plaster around it, old-timey numbers in pencil or scratched with a key, just three digits—*Ethel 468* or *Mamie 300*. I stroked a finger down the cool plaster and thought I could see a crowd of faces, all waiting alone in rented rooms for the bell to ring, for life to strike.

When we'd used up the space, we could hear the young woman knocking around in the kitchen. We found our way there and thanked her. She said shoot, she hadn't done nothing but rob us to see a dirty old house. She rushed on to add that she had a husband in the Army who was maybe coming home in two weeks, but I still doubt it. She had on the kind of cheap left-hand ring that girls have been known to buy from the dime store.

By then she was very much a girl to my eyes. And she had too lost a look in her eyes. This girl had been abandoned. When she told us that she'd have give us some dinner if she'd knowed we was coming, I felt like we ought to get out fast and neat. But Kevin kept asking her questions till it was clear she'd told the truth in one respect anyhow. She knew very little about the place—just that one of the Wolfes was famous and all, mostly up north as far as she could tell from the people that came, maybe ten on a weekday.

In fact as we finally turned to go, she asked me "Who was this fellow you're aiming at?" Though the visit was Kev's idea and he'd done most of the talking, she aimed her question straight at my eyes. And she seemed to be referring to Tom, as most native Tar Heels still call him, like a family member. I'd mentioned him at the start; and thinking she must admire him, I'd also said I was hoping to be as good at painting as Wolfe was at fiction. In fact I was hoping to be a lot better. So now I told her "He was one Asheville boy that wrote a famous book and died too soon."

She nodded as if she'd put that aside for further thought. Then she said "You find what you're looking for?"

I said "Well, it proves famous men can be born anywhere."

She said "Even stables." But then she laughed and apologized for the dust. "Seems like dust just dogs my tracks, every house I'm in. You could eat off'n my mama's floor, no plate. But look at all this." On its own, her hand indicated the floor—dust curled at our feet. Then she managed a smile, thanked us for coming and followed us to the door. The baby was no longer in sight. And when we were on the outside of the screen door, she stayed behind the rusty mesh.

But she made a last try. She laughed again, harder and covering her teeth. Then she said "You must not of gone to church either."

I confessed and said "Ain't it awful?" Back then in the South, if you missed Sunday church, you had you a good alibi before sunrise.

She stood there and genuinely fought with herself. It tortured her eyes. Then she said "They throwed me *out*, down there at Hog Elk—fine Christian souls!" Her last word flung on past us, towards the road.

Kev was plainly at a loss. This was a deeply Southern transaction, even though she was a mountaineer and I was piedmont. Many Americans would die naked in the road before they'd tell you what's hurt them the worst. But born Southerners will show you the cell in their heart that burns the hardest. They'll hold it right towards you, in their bare right hand. This girl had done that for me, Lord God. So what could I say but "That's all they know. You're far better off"?

Her thanks were deep and they welled in her eyes. But right away she said "Look, if you want to come back next week—both of you—and eat a good dinner I cook and all, you could read me some from that book he wrote. Then I'd know better what to tell folks. I feel real ignorant now." She dredged up her smile again, and this time it lasted so long I was ready to go back and better her lot by whatever means. With Father's death so raw in my heart, how could I leave a needy magnetic soul that pretty and lonesome?

Kevin was Yankee-polite about it—you know, you tell somebody the hard truth; but you tell it a little to the right of their eyes. Still he told her it just couldn't be. We were both tied up from here on out till summer ended. Then he took my elbow and steered me around.

Once I'd turned my back on her face, I couldn't look again. I might cave in and do something wild. Kev had seen that and done the right thing by me, mean as it seemed.

I can hear her voice though, clear as my own, right to this minute. "I hope people want to see your house someday."

WE SPENT THE REST OF SUNDAY EATING AND SEEING TWO movies. I said before that Kev was a true Yankee, from Rhode Island. He could no more ask you a personal question than flap his arms and fly unaided. Southerners ask intimate questions in the way monkeys groom each other for lice, not to pry but to make you feel cared for. Kev though could sit and stare, just past your ear for maybe five minutes, and not say a word. I could have robbed a bank vault and be wearing the Hope diamond in plain view, and he would have died before asking me about it. Since all my campers were children, and since their self-entrapment ruled out curiosity into lives older than their own, I was running a good two quarts low on close attention. So over the breaded veal cutlet at lunch, I said "I would have married that girl on the spot."

Kev said "So I noticed—girl and baby. Hope you didn't mind the rescue."

"Not a bit." But I did. I just slightly did.

Kevin said "I figured old Chief might be a little flummoxed if we got back tonight with a wife and baby." On other days off I'd told Kev a little about my presence at Father's death and, as I said, my ambitions. He'd heard me patiently and with what seemed genuine interest. He was hoping for a diplomatic career and would need a working knowledge of all brands of human folly. But as usual he asked no further questions.

So now I asked if he thought I was crazy.

He looked out the street window, in fact at the blinding sunlight, and said "Yes."

When I finished laughing I told him not to worry, that I was a little dizzy still from my hospital duties with Father, plus five weeks of boys, and would pipe down soon.

Kev waited and said "Don't get me wrong. You're beyond me now. You've seen a man die. And with no brothers or sisters, you're the last person in line in your family. That makes you the hitter and backstop and pitcher and all. You're rightly scared still."

It still seems a real piece of understanding. That it came from a twenty-one-year-old unmarried man, as protected as me, is hard to believe. I've never heard the same from anyone since, but I've noticed its accuracy in dozens of lives. Once you're the next member of your family in line for death, you become a new person. And for quite a while, you can easily fly off the handle and make entangling commitments or else you can run. We didn't say more on the subject that day, but I thought through it many times in the remainder of the summer. And I think it guided my subsequent actions. Which is not the same thing as blaming Kevin for my ignorant error.

WHEN WE GOT BACK TO CAMP PAST MIDNIGHT, THE AIR WAS actually cold. I walked into Cabin 16 thinking I'd be asleep in two minutes. But when I stripped and lay down, my mind was howling ahead. It mainly told me that the whole experience of the tawdry Wolfe house and the lost madonna

and child and Kevin's insight was a single shaft aimed at
my heart. I'd got both a big new wound and a gift—a broad
leap of knowledge that would show in my life, beginning
tomorrow. I had a fairly decent heart and a worthy aim. But
oh, I was loose in the world and must *work*.

My canvas was locked downhill in the crafts cabin, safe.
But at one in the morning, I halfway dressed and went down
there in the near freezing dark to study the drawing. At
night you tried to remember never to walk without a flashlight and to step high to avoid rattlers. So far this year nobody had been bit. The week before though, the hardy boys
from Tsali brought a full and squirming gunnysack down
the mountain. They said it was a dozen live rattlers they'd
trapped. They wanted undamaged skins to make hatbands
and belts, so they'd come up with the idea of gassing the
snakes by cranking the camp station wagon and tying the
mouth of the sack over the tailpipe. Without Chief's permission somehow they got the key, and the project very
nearly worked.

When the sack stopped moving, they turned off the engine, untied the sack and dumped the contents out on the
ground. I was there to see it. Sure enough, eleven dead
snakes. But the boys were sure there'd been twelve to start
with. They tried to recrank the engine and force the stray
out but the engine was dead. It turned out that the twelfth
snake had climbed up the tailpipe and got himself far forward in the exhaust system before dying in place. Chief
made the boys pool their spending money to get the station
wagon towed to Asheville where some brave fool located
the snake and fished it out. Of course all us city-slicker
counselors rejoiced at the downfall of the hard-scrabble Tsali

boys. But the gunnysack reminded me anyhow what kind of world was underfoot here, by day and night.

I got all the way to the crafts cabin safely and found the door unlocked. To rest his bowed legs, Uncle Mike kept a cot in the Indian lore room next door. I took the flashlight and went in to Mike's cot, propped my canvas on a chair and lay on my belly to study it. Even in black and white pencil line, I thought I could almost read the meaning of so much rock against so much sky. It was yearning to speak, the way a good dog—a setter or retriever—will meet your eyes and grieve, pure grieve, not to know your language.

If you think such thoughts are incompatible with good art, then you haven't read Michelangelo's poems or especially van Gogh's letters. They meant every picture as a forthright message, to change men's souls. Anyhow that night I was suddenly surer than ever that—if I was good and daring enough as a painter—I'd finish the summer with a picture that would also be a real gift of beauty and useful knowledge, for myself and every patient onlooker. Finally the whole good day fell on me. And lying under Mike's dusty Navaho blanket, I slid off to sleep and rested deeper than dreams or fears till cold first light.

Then Mike came limping through the door. With this stiff shock of white hair and his broad seamed face, he looked more than a little like pictures of God. And though he was older than Chief, he made at least as big a presence. When he finally saw me, he said "O Wise One, arise and dress. Seven new immortal souls await thee!" I had sat in on some of his Indian talks. He was genuinely informed on the subject, not just a half-baked enthusiast. And he'd taken to calling me Wise One because I also knew some Indian history.

I won't describe our many long talks. But from here looking back, I can see that Mike Dorfman was one of that summer's really good influences on my life. He'd graduated from Juilliard "back before God," as he said. Then he'd taken an M.A. in anthropology from Columbia, with fieldwork among two bands of the Sioux. And all this was forty years ago, just one generation after Wounded Knee and the Custer massacre. But the plight of the Indians disturbed him too deeply. So he turned aside, had a nervous breakdown—which he freely admitted to me—and spent his life teaching composition, piano, violin and "everything else but gynecology" at various conservatories and colleges. His wife had died young, leaving him with a daughter who was now somewhere with the Red Cross in Africa.

He'd met Chief in the late twenties, when he came down here to the Smokies to convalesce from TB. And once he retired from teaching, he decided to spend his summers at Juniper. That was mainly because it was so near the Cherokees. And also, he told me, because he had a whole lifetime of guilt to repay. He'd never forgiven himself for turning aside from the Sioux. He thought he could make some recompense by teaching white boys what a wrong we'd done, destroying the Indians. Since beginning to read I'd also consumed every word I could find on the same people, and I shared his guilt. If God is just, this country may never finish paying for their death—though maybe Vietnam was part of the payment, more or less exactly a century after our red version of a Final Solution. If so, at fifty thousand dead boys, we got off light.

Anyhow it was the first morning of second session and I'd overslept. I raced to shower and dress in my whites. Parents and new boys were driving towards us already from every corner of the South and a few from the Northeast. For the first time, I resented their droning nearness and my own renewed commitment to five more weeks of babysitting. A mind hot as mine, and aimed as narrowly, thought it needed whole days and weeks free to *see* and to translate. Or so I told myself, as I poised upright and old enough to know much better, on the doorsill of launching what may be the real piece of harm I've done the world.

IN THOSE DAYS EVEN MIDDLE-CLASS AMERICANS DIDN'T PICK up the long distance phone just to say "Good evening" to distant friends and ask what they might have had for dessert. Back then when you got a ring and picked up the receiver, that moment of staticky long distance noise would scare you cold—somebody was dead or deathly sick. But I'd promised myself for the past five weeks to call my girlfriend between the two sessions, also my mother. I'd written regularly to both, but voice is voice and I thought I was in special need of my girlfriend's. I haven't mentioned that I called her Viemme, our French pronunciation of her American initials V.M. She was apparently waiting table at a hotel on Mount Desert Island, Maine and had sent me a number for emergencies.

So that Sunday night I went down to the camp office. It was open to counselors by request for just such calls or for typing letters to campers' parents—"errands of mercy only," Chief had said. I thought I was being merciful to me; and I placed the call, charging it to Mother in Winston. *In seconds,* I thought, *this will all make sense. I'll send Mother a check before her bill comes; she'll understand.* But the phone in Maine sounded farther off than the Dalai

Lama's deepest cell. And as its ring bored on unanswered, I began to feel humiliated.

Here I'd spent two months with no sight, not to mention touch, of Viemme or any girl. I'd done serious work; we'd exchanged full letters, with my lyrical anatomical drawings that she responded to with a sonnet—what on Earth would I say? My mind whited out. I've mentioned that Viemme's cool good sense had stopped us from talking of eternal love. And we'd never ventured into the brand of long-distance pornographic transaction that some of the counselors informed me of. So what would we say?

Then I knew it didn't matter. Words weren't the point, for me anyhow, just her sound. I thought I needed the brief reminder that I still existed in a young woman's mind, that her hands recalled the times she'd taught me various grades of joy.

Finally a man's voice said "Mist Over."

At first I thought he was some sort of weather report I'd stumbled on by mistake—the rocky north coast, mist, nobody out tonight. Then I recalled "Mist Over" was the name of Viemme's hotel. So I asked for her.

The man took a long pause—Mother's bill was rising—and then he came back to say "Her roommate says she's spending the night where they don't have a phone."

I was more shocked by the fact of the news than by its contents. It was another long decade before American youth were that candid to strangers. For all the man knew, I was Viemme's father. What would these Yankees stop at, with their tact as raw as oysters? I thanked him anyhow and hung up firmly before I began to feel more than desolate. Granted that Viemme and I had agreed to be sensible about our time-bound relations. Still, when skin has been as mutually kind to skin as she and I had been, the sudden news that yet another whole suit of epidermis has been inserted literally between us—you know the feeling. Unspeakable sadness, followed by hot anger and cold disdain.

So I called Mother collect right away to head off the blues a few minutes longer. As usual she was sitting on the phone, with an instant cultivated "Hello." So we talked on for twenty minutes, a major financial commitment back then. At first I must have sounded preposterously official. Your distant son is making a courteous inquiry as to whether you're still breathing, madam. But her genius, and the secret weapon of all good mothers, was to pretend not to hear me and to plunge forthwith into a quiet and boring but deeply consoling narrative of the events of her daily life.

She started with how she went out to Aunt Sely's this morning to get the laundry and found Sely lying in the yard, with a broken hip and nothing but a blind dog for company. Sely had been there all night, Mother thought—of course it hadn't been terribly cold but still. Then Mother continued with how she rounded up some boys, and they got Sely into the car and safe to Bowman Gray Hospital. And how just tonight, just before I called, she'd come from the hospital where Sely was plaster-casted but happy, saying God had known—had flat out *knowed*—when to tame her pride. Sely had worked for us all through my parents' early marriage and then my childhood. And she'd quit awhile back on what she figured was more or less her eightieth birthday. But she'd insisted on washing our sheets till now. "Maybe this'll stop her finally," Mother said. "But don't bank on it. I'm *dying* to take my sheets to the laundry and get em pressed right. But Sely will rise from this, mark my word."

In five minutes she had me nodding in the old conspiracy

of mothers that of course *this* is the purpose and goal of life, not some heroic baying at the hazy moons of art and flesh. It was only when we'd played out all the events we could mention to one another that she took a little misstep and broke her spell. She said "Is your spending money holding out?"

Money of course was a joke this summer, my enormous salary. But I still had a fifty-dollar bank balance, and that would see me through another few book-buying trips to Asheville. I wasn't about to take funds from a working widow. I said "Yes, Mother. I'm solvent as a Vanderbilt."

She saw her mistake. "I knew that, Bridge. But I wanted to help."

Then I recovered my primal warmth long enough to get through a final restorative minute. I promised her that no, I didn't need her to come up and get me at the end of the month and that yes, I'd let her hear the moment anything went wrong.

She took a long pause, and I thought she was going to say she loved me—she generally did. I even braced for it. But she'd long since out-thought me. Or was just more honest. She said "I remember you plain as my father." Despite her father's early death, she loved him intensely to the end of her days. But what a strange and moving thing to say.

I was grateful at once and opened my mouth to let the spirit move me, and what came out still seems a fair match. I said "I remember you clear as the day I first saw you."

She laughed. "Well, damn! That was your first day."

I said "You're right."

AND JUST BEFORE DAWN I DREAMED OF HER BACK THEN— Mother, not Viemme or any other girl. In my mind for what

seemed hours of sleep, my mother wandered smiling beyond me, always near but just past reaching. She was young
as me now and wildly lovely, with long black hair that
bronzed in the light and eyes far deeper than any cave.

TWO

❖

MY SECOND ROUND OF BOYS LOOKED EVEN MORE manageable than the first. They were all on the smooth-cheeked side of puberty, and my newly honed scoutmaster skills served me better from the start. I could see that I met the anxious parents with more confidence and reassurance than before, so there were a minimum of whispered conferences on Jerry's constipation or Jake's ringworm. I knew now to say "We're well prepared for any problem, ma'm, though we don't expect any." One of my more easily acquired skills resulted from a tip of Chief's at an early counselors' meeting. He said "Any sentence delivered in a firm baritone or bass voice is automatically twice as forceful as the same exact words from a tenor or soprano." Now I met all comers successfully with my plummiest baritone. And I started the session with a private

promise to pay more personal notice to the campers and to
know them earlier.

The opening night campfire was held in the usual place,
the ring by the lake. It was a semicircular bowl of benches
around a sandy performance space, all set in a natural hill-
side covered with towering hemlocks. Siegfried or Beowulf
wouldn't have scorned to die there. It was that grand a setting, and all the human race had done for a change was to
make it slightly better. It was there that I first saw Rafe
Noren. I mentioned him far back at the start, and you may
have wondered where he went.

I hope you'll eventually understand how all this story is
more than partly about him. But his considerable presence
doesn't enter my life till here tonight, where he entered the
life of the second session. Because Rafe had spent most of
his childhood summers at Juniper, his talents were familiar
and precious to Chief. So he'd been asked to dance tonight,
last thing except for the prayer to Wakonda.

ONCE WE'D SUNG OUR WAY THROUGH THE FAMILIAR SONGS
and heard the old truths from Chief, Mike stood by the
dying fire and told us that the second session was to be
privileged by a three-week visit from Bright Day. Many of
the veteran boys cheered. Bright Day, Mike said, was a full-
blood Sioux from North Dakota. He was a nationally respected Indian expert and teacher. He'd recently testified
before Congress, and this would be his fifth year with us.
Even I, strapped as I was to my landscape, was curious to
test my Indian-book knowledge against blood experience.
Then Mike said that Ray Noren would conclude the evening
with his eagle dance. The veteran boys responded again but
without raucous cheers, more of a hushed reminder to

themselves. And Mike went to his seat in the front row of benches and began to beat slowly on a small tom-tom.

There was more light than the weak glow thrown by the fire—two small spots, high on trees—but as Rafe entered he drew all the shining directly his way. I've said he was fourteen and well along on his climb to physical maturity, but I doubt I can tell how serious an image he made on first sight. Whatever the state of his mind, he was already a young man, compressed into a body maybe five foot nine in height. He wore only a beaded deerskin breechclout, a porcupine-quill roach on his head, bands of iron bells on his ankles and wrists and wings of dark gray feathers on his arms.

I'd watched various dance companies as they passed through Winston or Chapel Hill or on occasional trips to New York. I'd even seen the Sadler's Wells Ballet with Margot Fonteyn. And towards the end of *Cinderella*, she did something the human body absolutely can't do. She was balanced far forward on her right point. Then instantly without visibly moving, she switched feet and was poised way forward at exactly the same angle, still as a resting bird, on her left point. So I had some notion of what dancing could be.

But within a minute of soaring around that ring and those coals, Rafe Noren managed in my mind what no other performer of anything had managed. He became a nocturnal eagle—that self-sufficient, that strong. He was riding the drafts of a summer night, oblivious of us. You'll grant, I trust, that for an adolescent boy to achieve an air of credible brute majesty is unlikely on a phenomenal scale. Yet Shakespeare's boy actors had to be capable of just such a reach. Think of Lady Macbeth, Cleopatra, Goneril and Regan.

Rafe Noren did at least as much, if not more. Once he'd brought off a real metamorphosis, he then held us with him. And we were two dozen adults and a hundred cold children, well past their bedtime. We watched intent through maybe four minutes till the drumbeat slowed and the eagle's wings locked full out for a glide to Earth. That was his perch in the ring at our feet.

Will I sound crazier still if I say that it didn't occur to me that he was a boy again till people started clapping and he stood up? I was glad anyhow he didn't break down into grins and bows. He nodded his unsmiling head one time and then somehow vanished from the ring. On his two feet surely, though I don't recall. In the years since, I've seen Olivier eight times and Gielgud more still. I've seen Vanessa Redgrave, Nureyev, Martins and Baryshnikov. I've heard Flagstad and Melchior, Callas, Bjoerling and Price and was grateful to them all. But it's only the simple truth to say that I never saw but one actor *change* into what he meant to be—change and stay there as long as he wanted to and keep you with him—and that was Rafe Noren.

BY THE TIME WE WERE BACK IN CABIN 16, I'D LEARNED A few facts from one of my veteran boys. Ray was Raphael, from south Georgia. He was fourteen and "well-known" wherever Juniper boys lived.

When I asked if Rafe did anything but dance, my boy thought an instant and laughed. "He can turn his eyelids inside out. Worst-looking thing you ever saw! One boy got sick last year when he did it at supper, and Mrs. Chief told Ray not to ever do it again or he'd go blind and be expelled from camp, both."

The news didn't make or break my night. I mean, I

charged up the metamorphosis more to my own highly tuned senses than to any uncanny skill in Rafe.

AND IT WAS THE THIRD DAY BEFORE I SAW HIM AGAIN. LIKE college students, the boys shopped around in the morning classes before settling on what they'd pursue for the rest of the month. I had my art class already grounded with drawing boards before a new boy drifted in. With remarkable self-possession he began to tour the room, silently judging the work. He was making no disturbance, and I had no idea that he'd been the eagle dancer.

But finally I went over and asked if he was interested in the class.

He said "Oh sir, I was looking for you. A couple of the other old boys have told me you're somebody to know."

Flattery is something you almost never get from children. Since you never give them enough of anything they need, they have no reason to overpraise you. So I took him at his word—there were three or four ten-week campers in the older cabins; they might have told him. I said "You want to practice your seeing skills? Get you some supplies and start drawing that bowl of rocks. I'll check you in a few minutes."

He said "One question, please sir. I've heard of drawing bowls of fruit or flowers but a bowl of rocks?" No smile at all.

I said "They were what I had. Try to imagine they're edible. Any painter's got to learn to eat what's before him."

He thought and then grinned. "Oh they're nutritious. I been eating them for years, and look how I've grown." Then he said "Is there something I sign to stay here, like a class roll?"

I told him I wasn't that formal, but what was his name?

Some faceless voice at the back of the room boomed "RAY-feel."

He held out his hand to me and said "Raphael Noren."

All I'd heard that first night was the name Ray Something, so this name still didn't dawn on me. I said "Can I call you Rafe?"

He laughed. "Oh lord, please do. Everybody else calls me Ray, and that just gives me the fantods. I been aiming at Rafe for countless ages. Don't it sound like a riverboat gambler?"

I said "Sure does but I didn't know anybody had the fantods since Huck Finn."

"And me, Rafe Noren—not but ten times an hour." He grinned and went about finding his supplies.

In a quarter hour I checked by his stool. On the big piece of clean newsprint, he had already outlined the subject. Just by judgment of the eye, he had transferred the deep bowl and the various stones to his paper in almost perfect one-to-one scale. That is, his drawing was precisely the size of the subject. He had no way of knowing, but he'd employed almost identically the same method I used in my underdrawing for the mountain landscape. He employed a strong sinuous line with no shading, something like a classical-period Picasso drawing. To be sure I was immediately struck by the coincidence and said "Have you seen the painting I just started?"

Rafe kept working but said "No, are you a painter too?"

Bowled a little off-center, I laughed and said "What do you think my main line is?"

"Oh I meant you being a counselor up here, checking on pissy mattress pads and ticks."

Summer boys were a little less respectful than boys in schooltime, but in general I'd had a good deal of respect at Juniper. Now the boys around us, who'd pretended not to listen, exploded in giggles. Somebody had bowled the teacher over. Pandemonium spread. So Rafe and I joined them, and I brought out my canvas. That slowly calmed things.

Rafe looked for a long minute, which was a marathon study as children's looks go, and said "That's always been my favorite too."

"Favorite what?"

"View, the best thing to watch at Juniper. My father says there's a sermon in it, all those rocks in the sky."

Just as I was on the verge of rushing in with the further astounding coincidence—how I also sensed a coded message in that horizon line—Rafe said "But he sees a sermon in a pile of dog do."

A brief return of chaotic glee, though some of the boys were also showing signs of envy. Rafe was getting too much of my time, so I told him to keep drawing. And then I patrolled the room again, praising the knotted or swollen other efforts.

When the time came to stop for lunch, everybody else pounded away. But Rafe was still at the back, intent at his board.

I tidied up and finally asked him to come forward, show me his day's work and wash his hands for lunch.

He was genuinely unready to stop and kept on drawing for another few minutes.

Finally I had to say "*Time* there, boy. I'm hungry."

When he sprang up in place and faced me with the nearest thing to fury I've seen on a child's face, I suddenly

recognized him. Or maybe I saw the core of power in him
that had turned into an eagle as he danced. Anyhow it was
my first experience of how an offstage face can differ from
the limelit mask. Have you ever seen photographs of Nijin-
sky offstage? The randy ethereal faun became a semimon-
goloid shoeshine boy. And Rafe Noren by daylight was a
good-looking American boy but not what he'd been by
drumbeat at night.

He didn't want me to look at his drawing. I insisted and
then I saw to my surprise that for the past half hour he'd
been working on an unnervingly intricate abstract frame
around all four sides of his original line drawing. I said
"Don't you believe in shading? Things do have dimensions,
you know." I stopped for fear of his giving me some extra-
planetary truth about dimensions.

Rafe just said "I can't stand to get things dirty." Then
calmly he took the paper from my hands and tore it four
ways. Matter of factly, not angrily.

I said "I like for all my boys to keep a file of their work.
Then you can show your parents how far you've pro-
gressed."

Rafe said "My father wouldn't care if I was God."

I laughed but smelled a broken home. "They know you're
an eagle."

Rafe looked puzzled and for an instant I thought I'd mis-
identified him. But then he gave his sunrise-over-the-Grand-
Canyon grin. It was that wide and welcome. He said "That
is all right, idn't it?" I'll hint occasionally at his Georgia
accent. Before I could think *Stuck-up little bastard*, the grin
collapsed disastrously, then comically. His two big upper
front teeth fell down from the gum and rested on his lowers,
leaving a big black gap in his face.

He'd lost the teeth in a junior-high football accident. The collapsible plate was temporary, till his jaw reached mature size. So he'd quickly learned to use it as a deflationary stunt to clear the air around him whenever it thickened.

Once I recovered from the shock, I asked what he planned to be, as a man.

He said "Not you too."

I said "O.K., not me. I just wondered if you were going to keep on with your dancing?"

He said "I could quit that dancing *now*. I just do it for Bright Day and Uncle Mike. Mike's been good to me since I was six years old, and Day taught me all I know about dancing."

I told him that, from what I saw last night, I'd guess he had something better than a teacher could give. But I also said I was sure Day was proud.

Rafe said simply, "If he is, he never told me."

I said "Aren't Indians famous for not talking a lot?"

He said "Every one I know talks a blue damned streak."

I was going to ask how he knew so many Indians and whether he danced anywhere but Juniper, in the summer.

But he suddenly remembered a man's round wristwatch on his arm. "Lord, I told a boy I'd fight him."

Before I could ask what he meant or say "It's time for lunch," he tore off like a greyhound.

ALL THE LOCAL WAYS TO DESCRIBE RAFE NOREN CALLED for animal comparisons. Everybody who really knew him understood that. Not that he inspired the talentless to flights of eloquence. But you couldn't help noticing the things people called him—simple things like "quick as a deer," "smart as a fox," "lean as a snake." But the important thing to keep reminding myself and you is, none of us seemed to think of him as anything very exceptional, certainly not anything poetic. Not yet. If people commented on Rafe at all, it was usually just to say his dancing improved every year; and wasn't he growing up too fast? The older people all mentioned his manners—how polite he was, what an eager smiler.

In the second week, my seventh of the summer, Mrs. Chief called me to her one day by the lodge and said "I see Ray Noren's honored you."

I must have looked puzzled.

"You're his favorite this year. He's hard to please. But I trust his choices. Be good to him, hear?"

I assured her I would.

She said "Extra good" and held her eyes on mine uncomfortably long.

To break her hold I looked to the ground and started to tell her about his drawings, how he still insisted on bareline drawing.

But she touched my arm and dropped her voice. "If that causes trouble—if Ray gives you any trouble at all, Bridge, come to me first."

I actually laughed.

But she was dead earnest. She gave my forearm the kind of smack you expect in grade school. Then she said "Did you hear me?"

I was cowed. "Yes ma'm."

Finally she smiled. "I hoped I could trust you." Then she blinked hard and turned. Mrs. Chief was so broadbeamed, she didn't so much walk away as steam or sway on off downhill in a regal progress.

But as she moved I wondered about her main advice. *Be*

good to Ray. Who hadn't been? Was there something to know?

DAYS WENT ON, THE WAY DAYS DO. AND I WENT FURTHER ahead with my painting. I developed that summer a tactic I've used ever since. When I'm bringing a complicated image forward, I generally work in the classic Renaissance manner. With an almost infinite number of thin color glazes or washes, I work steadily from left to right. Then I throw myself back left again like an old typewriter and start all over. I don't jump at random, coloring a whole tree here or a rockface there, however tempting such detours are. My old way can be agonizingly slow, but at least the whole picture looks more or less finished at the end of each day. In fact my single most difficult decision comes in knowing when to stop burying yesterday's picture in today's new thoughts.

Choosing consciously, I set my vantage point on the terrace just outside the crafts cabin. So once I got my class to work every morning, I could move outside with my own picture; and the boys could follow or go to some other point of their choice. They just brought me their work at the end of class, and I gave them my comments and corrections. Sad to say, despite my constant urging to loosen up, open up, draw from the elbow and not the cramped hand, very few of the boys improved in any useful way.

Even a boy as intelligent as Rafe was hard to teach. He couldn't agree to corrupt the purity of two-dimensional drawing. He was genuinely opposed, as I said, to the usual methods of shading. From his point of view they just "dirtied up a clean thing." Since all the known methods do generally require an artist to smudge with a finger, or at least to stipple with the pencil or brush, Rafe was technically right. I tried to teach him alternate methods, but there was no real library at Juniper.

So I couldn't show him examples of the elegant linear shading in Leonardo or the swift crosshatching in Rembrandt. In Rembrandt's drawings and especially his etchings, whole mysterious threats of darkness are implied by nothing but what looks like hen scratch till you slow down and wait. Then his world begins to be charged with demons in hiding in the shade. I tried to draw samples for all the boys, and three of them halfway got the point.

But Rafe's work stayed in the outline stage. Though his outlines improved in speed and obedience to the actual boundaries of objects, he never promised to deal adequately with a world of infinite shades.

And after I said "Shade!" for the hundredth time, he shot me a lethal glare and said "Over your dead body."

I laughed but he didn't, so I left it there and accepted his outlines.

Anyhow I had to keep reminding myself what an achievement Rafe managed as it was, he or any of the other boys. I mean, it's fairly incredible—right?—that you can set a random dozen humans to copy an egg on a plate, and they'll all come up with a picture that most other people can name. An egg on a plate, or at worst a white rock or a golf ball. Think of those stupendously complex light rays passing intact through space, through a dozen brains, down arms, through hands and fingers onto paper. They've almost got gorillas trained to do it. Any day now, any day.

The world's outlines almost never behave the way people think they do. For instance go into an otherwise empty room and try to draw your mate's profile from memory. Ludicrous clearly. Now come out, study his or her face for a minute, then draw the profile again. You'll almost certainly make as many serious mistakes the second time as the first. And all your mistakes will come where you *assume* that the line of her upper lip is concave like *this* when in fact it's convex like *that*. If I taught anything at Juniper, I hope it was this. *Keep your eye on the object*, or it will trick you and keep its own secrets. For secrets are what the whole visible world tries constantly to keep, for some mysterious reason.

The main other good thing I did was to work on my own picture in the presence of the boys. I'd get them started and check in on them every quarter hour or so. Otherwise I'd be at my own job, among them. And all but one or two of the spiritually blind spent long silent minutes every day, watching my progress. I had to strain not to condemn the ones who never looked. But even today I'll have to admit I divide the world, one way at least, into the dozen who notice what's hanging on the walls and the billion who don't. Rafe Noren never let a class end without stopping by for a dignified look. No comment usually, or a low pleased grunt. But oh I knew I'd already burned that mountain line on one brain at least.

WHATEVER ELSE I DID WRONG THAT SUMMER—AND IT WAS plenty—I managed to paint one sizeable picture, thirty-six by twenty. And a lot of people, young and old, watched me make it from hour to hour. I never said a word about what drew me to the subject, my half-shamed guess at a pregnant horizon. They all just assumed that a fine view was obvious fodder for any artist—every sofa needs a view. More than one of them asked me if I would sell it to them at the end.

I always refused politely, saying I meant to keep it as my

souvenir of the summer. It didn't seem to break any hearts. At least nobody asked for it twice except Rafe. He found a new way more or less daily to intimate that a gift of the painting to the Raphael Noren Art Museum would be graciously received. I'd just laugh and fend him off one more time. Even then he made my favorite remark of the summer about it.

After one of his more dogged efforts to wangle the painting, he said "I just want something somebody loves as much as I can see you love this picture."

And I still have it, at the head of my bed in a long sand-colored room where I've spent more than half the nights of my life. I've kept it because it's the first really decent accomplishment in all my work and also because, as I predicted, it turned out to be—in the last way I'd have planned—a souvenir of my summer as a counselor, an almost adequate receptacle for all my memories, good and tragic.

I can't reproduce it here for you, so I'm asking you to take my word that it's an honorable reminder of a big experience in the presence of an even bigger beauty. Whether you like American neorealist landscapes or not, I honestly think you'd be impressed by this one or at least detained for a reasonable look. God knows, the man who painted it was impressed. He really watched one stretch of the world, through a long run of good days. You can feel his attention.

What it also shows me, and anyone else who knows my work, is that for the first time in my life, I had the means to say what I felt. Whether or not you consciously sense a mysterious purpose—my try at conveying a silent tongue—is not that important. Lots of intelligent people look at Vermeers and see homely Dutch house-daughters standing in window light, doing odd jobs; and they love what they see. They feel rewarded for the minute or two they stand and look, which is no small gift.

The same with me and mine. If you see "The Smoky Mountains as the Meaning of Things" and just remember a restful weekend three years ago with the wife and children in a rented camper on the Blue Ridge Parkway, fine by me. The title of the picture to be sure is the thing I'm uneasy about now, but it's the name I gave it at the time, so I go on owning up to that much fervor in the young man who wore my name that summer.

OTHERWISE THE SECOND SESSION WENT LIKE THE FIRST. UP at seven to a distant bugle, brush your teeth, eat breakfast, teach morning classes, a big lunch, then a rest hour in the cabins, an hour's work on *The Thunderbird* or Indian lore, then a swim in the frigid lake or tennis, clean up, eat supper, then campfire or a program in the lodge, brush teeth again, taps at nine and a final hour or so with the other counselors in our private clubhouse. With the arrival of Bright Day at the end of the second week, I tactfully satisfied myself on his sincerity and genuine knowledge. He also had an M.A. in anthropology, from the University of North Dakota. So I spent a lot of afternoons with him in the Indian lore room of the crafts cabin.

First he'd give a brief lesson on some aspect of Plains Indian life, nothing too long to bore the boys. Then he'd break us down into small working groups and rotate around us. He'd guide the boys who were beading headbands or making breechclouts or full-dress war bonnets. There was a ten-dollar surcharge for the felt base, beads and turkey feathers that went into a bonnet. Eagle feathers were way too expensive, though nobody had yet thought much about the eagle as an endangered species.

Day was a normal-sized gentle but unsmiling man in maybe his early thirties. His profile and huge dark eyes linked him instantly to his forebears. His grandfather, whom he remembered, had been one of the war chiefs in the Custer massacre at the Little Bighorn in 1876. And more than once Day told us what he recalled of the old man's stories. For instance at the end of the battle, Day's grandfather found a compass on one of the dead cavalrymen. However he turned it, the needle always pointed one way. So Grandfather understandably thought it was magic and predicted that more white soldiers would come from the direction of the needle. A few of the loose bands of warriors regrouped, headed north and sure enough met and damaged a troop coming to Custer's rescue.

I've mentioned my old Indian sympathies. Even at childhood cowboy-and-Indian movies, I knew to root for the Indians. They were in so much better shape, and talk about better riders—bareback with no stirrups! In photographs they also had the absolutely frank faces I couldn't help drawing, over and over. Any pair of their eyes said nothing less than *Take me or kill me but I belong here*. I'd also gathered, from reading and from my own love of the land we lived on, that after all every American Indian was here before any of us and that none of the paleface alibis covered the evil that had followed and continues.

So I was all the more susceptible to Bright Day's poker-faced narratives, however legendary some may have been. And I gladly planked down the ten-dollar fee to make my own bonnet. Like most only children I've got the born craftsman's love of manual labor. Seated on the floor near

Day, and surrounded by high-voiced children, I could bury myself pretty well forever in a meticulous trance of gluing, sewing and beading. Up till then I'd had a tendency to unbidden visits by the dreadful scenes of my father's last days.

I'd suddenly see him tearing out all his intravenous needles and crouching under the bed, blood streaming. When I asked him, he'd say he was hiding from the nurses who were coming to cut him. Or in the midst of calling instructions to a camper, I'd hear Father bellowing "No, no" at the mute hallucinations of his nights. When I asked him once to say what he saw, he said again "*No.* It's for *me* to bear." But huddled on the floor of Day's calm room or alone with my painting, I was always at more than arm's length from the worst. And when the scenes returned at all, I could see they were fading.

It apparently had something to do with the fact that all artisans are blessed with what I call bleeding hands. Through their fingers—painting, sculpting, writing, hammering or through a dancer's feet—artisans can bleed off each morning all the night's log jam of blame and dread. So I gave both my manual jobs all the time I didn't give my boys. I even passed up a couple of days off to stay at Juniper, painting and beading. That of course was seen by the staff as an awesome sign of devotion, also lunacy.

NEEDLESS TO SAY RAFE WAS ANOTHER INDIAN LORE ENthusiast. He'd already made a bonnet and all the other authentic-looking paraphernalia of his dances, so he was well ahead of the rest of us. This summer with Day's guidance he was beading a pair of soft buckskin moccasins with white and sky-blue Czechoslovakian beads. For some reason the world's best Indian beads are made there, in gentle

colors and uniform sizes. Rafe would seldom talk when he
was working, but he did say he was hoping to wear the new
moccasins in this year's closing-night ceremonies, so he
worked with a calm kind of intensity. And always in a corner sat Clara Jenkins. She was Chief's sweet-natured old-
maid niece, maybe forty. And she was stitching twenty ghost
shirts on an ancient foot-pedaled Singer machine.

Bright Day had decided that the centerpiece of closing
night was to be a repetition of the Ghost Dance. The original dance had been the tragic hope of a Paiute Indian seer
named Wovoka. Late in the 1800s he taught various tribes
a peaceful dance to be performed in long white shirts that
he said would render them impervious to harm. The dance,
rightly performed, would result in the coming of an Indian
messiah. And that wondrous creature would harmlessly dis-
pel the cruel and wasteful white man. Then he'd establish a
new order among his own people. The Ghost Dance spread
rapidly through the plains and soon alarmed the ignorant
U.S. Cavalry who attempted to suppress it. The Indian hope
was too bright though. The dance and the struggle continued till both reached a ghastly impasse at Wounded Knee,
South Dakota in 1890. There the scared soldiers killed more
than two hundred Sioux whose white shirts proved all too
pervious to bullets, though the dance continues even today
among a dwindling group of the hopeful. Or so my *Britan-
nica* says.

The Indian lore boys then, two other counselors, Clara
and I would sit quietly working through the sun-struck August afternoons, listening to the soft and cultivated voice of
Bright Day as he described our roles in closing night. First
would come the lighting of the small peripheral fires that
each of the cabins had built beforehand. Then Rafe would

dance, to draw the benign notice of the Great Spirit. Uncle Mike and Day would sing some appropriate songs and prayers. Then Chief would speak. And to end the summer, the rest of the boys in Day's class would put on Clara's ghost shirts and close the night by pressing on the Spirit for rescue.

It didn't seem to occur to anybody but me that the tortured past of the Ghost Dance made it a peculiar, if not a dangerous, culminating event. Who were we hoping to drive away? What kind of messiah did we have in mind? And what about all the blood that flowed at the start of the dance? Day was friendly, with the slow dignity of a member of a species closely related but not quite the same as mine. Yet despite the fact that I talked with him daily, I couldn't bring myself to reveal my uneasiness. Somehow I knew that he wasn't staging the dance as a straight historical recollection. He had some hope invested in it still. So I chalked the anxiety up to my brittle inner weather and kept it to myself, with one exception.

On an afternoon when Day seemed unusually relaxed, I reminded him that there was a National Guard armory just down the road. And I said "What if the cavalry hears about this? We could end up dead."

Day very nearly laughed. But once he got his face composed, he said "We could also end up saved."

And Rafe, who was beading nearby, said "I don't know which would be worse."

SO WITH ART CLASS AND INDIAN LORE, I SPENT TIME EVERY day around Rafe. Up through the second week, he and I had no specially close relation. He was in Kevin's group of senior boys, two cabins farther up the mountain from mine.

The distance between Kev's fourteen-year-olds and my younger boys was miles longer than the fifty real yards of ground. To be sure I kept my memory of Rafe's eagle dance. I respected his odd compunctions in art class, and I was increasingly conscious of the other rare qualities I've mentioned. But so was everybody. A human being who steadily glows with something more than greeting-card light is not daily issue in anybody's life, and all of us knew it.

He dived, swam, wrestled and played baseball with good-natured abandon if not with the skill of his dancing. The fact that there were better athletes in every sport helped all of us like Rafe better. It assured everybody he was one of us. And I think he knew it. Whenever he failed to catch a pop fly or got knocked over in a boxing match, he almost overplayed the role of goofy loser. He plainly loved to think he was normal and would grow up to be nothing better or worse than a happy man. But however much he downplayed his dancing, if you remembered you hadn't seen Rafe for a day or so, you could always loop by the campfire ring. Chances were, he'd be there dancing—*dancing* not rehearsing.

For he never broke off to correct himself or ever looked up at any spectator but went straight on with whatever urgent business his limbs transacted. On behalf of whom and with what for money and what were the stakes? He was always on the verge of becoming the golden boy of the summer, except that we saw how mercilessly he teased himself and how reluctant we were to join in laughing at a boy who understood this early that his was a sacrificial life.

ONE AFTERNOON I'D FINISHED MY *THUNDERBIRD* STINT early and was poking around. The lake was full of the youngest and loudest boys, so I bypassed that and walked over to the ring to check. Sure enough Rafe was there, in khaki shorts and no shirt, dancing. I thought that, since it seemed plainly a rehearsal, I could talk. So at several points I commented on this or that step.

Nothing showed I was bothering him. But without breaking rhythm, he finally said "Bridge, I'm dancing. Talk to me later."

I sat back chastened and waited while he ended whatever he was doing—something pertaining to the center of the ring, where fires were built.

Eventually he worked his way to the center and wound up prostrate there, arms out, away from me. He stayed still a moment, then broke his own spell, leapt up, walked over and asked if I wasn't playing hooky. There was sand all down his chest and arms.

"Not hooky exactly. I've finished up the very next *Thunderbird* and am airing my brain."

Rafe said he'd send his brain with me next time, for ventilation.

I recalled how he'd turned aside my question about his future, but I thought the air felt different today, and I risked a new question. "How did you learn the way to do this, Rafe?"

He stared towards the lake for maybe ten seconds, raising both hands to his face for a moment. "Angel messengers," he finally said. Then he turned back to me with both eyelids rolled inside out and a wide open grin, with dropped upper plate.

ON THE SUNDAY THAT BEGAN THE THIRD WEEK OF SECOND session, a strong chain began to show its links. That morn-

ing we had a guest preacher up at the Pasture. He was a
startling sight, with lank snow-white hair parted in the middle and hanging to his shoulders. There it was hacked off
brutally even. If you've seen photographs of the old Franz
Liszt, you'll know the style. It made our preacher look far
and away the oldest man I'd seen. If he'd had a beard, he'd
have been a dead ringer for Santa Claus's granddad.

Yet though Father's Day was behind us, he asked our
permission to speak about fathers. I mean he literally gazed
out at our many faces and focused hotly on one, then another. At last he said "Boys and counselors, I have a *need*
to share my own heart's burden with you. Chief Jenkins tells
me that, as recently as June, he spoke with you on the
subject of fathers. But I wasn't here that blessed morning.
I was at the bedside of my own dying father, deeper on up
in the mountains near Glendale Springs. Since then at the
great age of ninety-six, he has passed on over. I need to
tell you about that. Will you grant me permission to talk
about fatherhood and its divine blessings?"

My cabin mates were huddled around me. All seven faces
looked up with expressions of comic weirdness. *His father's
got to be older than the wheel. Who does he think he's
fooling?*

So I had to join the feeble chorus of audible yeses. Everybody urged this mutant to speak.

He gave his own age first, which was seventy-four. His
father had made it to ninety-six in fine fettle, right up to
this past May. Then the old gentleman took a mighty tumble
down two flights of steps, down one and somehow right on
across the landing and then down the second. Understandably he felt poorly for the experience. So he summoned his
only live child—our speaker—and proceeded to weaken fast.

On the second night he lapsed into a profound coma. More than one bystander said he was dead, but our guest preacher wouldn't let them haul him out. He said there was hope, and he sat a loyal vigil at the bedside. Then after sixteen unbroken hours, sure enough, the old man opened both eyes, sat bolt upright and asked for a breakfast of scrambled eggs, grits and fried Vienna sausages.

When he'd eaten every mouthful, the old gentleman took our preacher by the hand and said "Ottis, hear me. I wasn't asleep. I was dead and in Heaven, whence I saw your patient devotion down here. The main thing to know is, Heaven's not a place flooded with light like they say or with all that music and famous song. It's restfully still and dim as a starlit Cuban night"—he'd been in the Spanish-American War—"but otherwise it's far more wondrous than promised. I never would have left, but they sent me back since you're a preacher. They said 'Tell your boy and make him pass it on.' So now I've told you and can go back to bliss." With that the old gentleman fell back, truly dead.

And that was it. Except for a few inadequate words of interpretation and local application, the sermon was over. The preacher thanked us for hearing his news. He said never forget it, and then he raised his long arms in blessing. Mike Dorfman rose to pitch the last hymn and could barely conceal a gorgeous grin. Even Chief, who rose to say the last prayer, seemed two degrees warmer with either delight or mortification.

MY BOYS OF COURSE ALL TOOK IT IN STRIDE. IT WAS JUST outrage number two million, twenty-four by the adult race in the past two days. They did want to know at the lunch table if—it being in church and all—that meant the preacher's story was true?

By then the comic overtones were fading. Despite the fact that the preacher was sitting beside Mrs. Chief this minute, bolting down chicken, there'd been something in his exotic aura that was rising inside me now like iridescent oil or the pulsing colors of a hummingbird's throat. I suddenly felt he'd been speaking to me, outrageous as he was with his hair and his loony unvarnished but oddly credible message. He'd at least thrown light on my own father's life. That life, for the moment, was safe in the starry dark he described.

That'll seem unworthy now, a ridiculous deduction from a more than normally nutty pulpit claim. I can only trust that some of you—even in a time of almost universal hospital deaths—have experienced a similar loss, deepened by long hours of vigil on bitter sights. If so, you've probably shared my rocky equilibrium in succeeding months. You'll recall the flashbacks, the endless heart-stopping dreams in which you discover your dead loved one, alive and well, on the far side of the room at a party. You say to yourself "*Wait*. Didn't they tell me that Father had died? Of course they did but—look—there he is, laughing and strong. They must have been wrong. Can I dare to believe it?"

Anyhow in the midst of seven boys, baked chicken, mashed potatoes and peas, I was suddenly moved. I opened my mouth to answer the question—maybe the old man's guess about Heaven was good as any—but words wouldn't come. I didn't go on to howl or stream tears. I was just mute and a little misty.

The boys all knew about my father, so they halfway understood my reaction and treated me kindly, with a certain awe. *Whoa, one more grownup is showing a* feeling. *Better watch this closely.* The youngest boy, Battle Beecham, even managed to pat the back of my hand. No laughter, no questions.

I'll forever be grateful. And long before we finished dessert, I was clear again and laughing. I told the boys to run to the cabin and start their nap while I detoured to speak to the guest.

I went to Chief's table and shook the preacher's enormously long hand. He was one of the old-fashioned Protestant handshakers who wouldn't release your hand. This one's hand was warm and dry; most hand captors are cold and moist. I've honestly forgot his last name, but I could sketch you a speaking likeness of his face and mimic his sepulchral voice.

He insisted on standing and drawing off a quart or so of my energy through the eyes. Then at last he said "You especially wanted that news—am I wrong? *Am I wrong?*"

I assumed that Chief had told him my background. I also knew that the only hope of escape was to nod, say yes and thank him again.

He held my hand still, in the lengthening silence. That was another of the great Protestant emotional events, a not-blinking match. He was trying to return, through open eyes, all that he'd drained off me half a minute ago.

So I took it, smiling.

Then he said "Bridge—what a wondrous name! Bridge, you pass this news on too. It's why I'm alive here, old as I am. That selfsame news will keep you alive, if you use it a-right."

At last I could feel his grip relax. My hand slid free, though bloodless and numb. I said again "Thanks" and walked away, grinning slyly at Meshach, the black busboy who'd watched my plight.

He pointed to my hand and whispered "Go rinch it off quick, Bridge—real hot water—else it'll *wither*."

I laughed and told him I would. But all the way uphill in sunlight, through white-clad boys playing tetherball and chiseling grotesque totem poles to leave here behind them, I knew I halfway believed the story and would pass it on.

THAT NIGHT AFTER TAPS, THE COUNSELORS MET IN THE parlor. That was a dim room off the dining hall, meant apparently for entertaining parents but almost never used. Chief had put up a note requesting our presence two weeks ago and rumors had flown. It was everybody's fondest hope that this was to be Chief's famous annual sex talk. But in view of the easiness of our work in the second session, and our running good luck with health and welfare, that seemed almost too good to be possible.

Wrong. When all fourteen of us were seated—all male, all single, all under twenty-five—Chief rose with his usual high sheen of purpose. He began with an unusually relaxed paragraph of thanks for our help in the summer's success to date. But being Chief of course he suddenly ended the relaxation with a realistic reminder—"As the good darkies say, 'Don't call yourself happy till you're propped up dead in dry shoes and socks.'"

Then he went on to praise our health, the clarity of our skin, the forthrightness of our smiles and handshakes. Anyone our age knew that he was telling us, in the universal anatomical code of the time, that he believed us to have torn free—by sheer force of will and faith, here in the unmatched air of Juniper—of the ever-ready toils of masturbation. I've said before that he was wrong about me in that respect, among others. And the rapidly sinking level of confessional humor in the counselors' cabin indicated that I was far from alone.

Next he said it had come to his attention that two of us were to be married soon. It was his conviction that all of us would in good time join the Earth's privileged band of the happily wed. Till then however his own experience gave him ample reason to know with what pitfalls and trials we'd be faced. And he therefore hoped that we could suspend our natural modesty and permit him to pass on to us his own gleanings from life.

I won't make further fun of an honestly but ludicrously out-of-touch effort to help. Suffice to say that Chief took us through an anatomy lesson that might have enlightened a five-year-old. Then he proceeded through the ethical and theological bases for chastity before and occasionally *during* marriage. And he ended in an effort to combine further information with a proof of his good-guy nature. He told the old salesman's story of the innocent and overeager groom who terrifies his bride so badly with the sight of his aroused and ruddy glory that she only just permits his entry. But then as he nears the pearly effusion, she locks down with all her iron muscles and traps him so inescapably that the hotel doctor must be summoned with relaxing morphine before the groom can be freed.

He'd delivered the body of his speech with blue eyes fixed on a stag's head hung on the wall behind us. The fact that he now gazed down and met us head-on, eye by eye, surely meant he was moving toward an end. I was torn between relief and disappointment—thank God it's over but don't let it end. He again referred to the marriage of two among us.

He trusted that the honeymoons of both would profit from this private hour. He trusted that the remainder of us would profit in time. That rich reward would inevitably follow if we pursued the principles outlined here tonight. Then and then only would our virgin bodies discover, with our God-given mates, "the highest joy this Earth can afford—the sight of your God-meant loved one's eyes as she meets you, transfixed in ultimate union and joy by your pure tool."

OR "POOR FOOL" AS WE NAMED IT WHEN WE'D ALL RUSHED back to the counselors' cabin for an incredulous recap. Reports from veteran counselors and years of rumor—nothing could have prepared us for the bonanza Chief unloaded. Being, as we were, a pivotal generation between the old and new brands of American sexuality, Victorian and free, we'd heard more than a few bizarre sermons on the subject. But to a man, we gladly conceded that Chief's contribution, at one swell foop, had trumped all contenders. And in full awareness of early reveille racing toward us, we nonetheless sat up punitively late, fixing the evidence deep in our memories.

ALONE FOR A SHORT TWO MINUTES THOUGH, ON THE PITCH-black walk to my cabin, I knew I'd made a childish mistake. Too many older men had helped me, with their generous minds and affections—my father, my surviving grandfather, Mother's two brothers, three of my college professors. In the cold night I saw Father plain, the last time I was home before his attack. He'd paid for a new dark blue suit for me and had phoned me at college to say the alterations were ready, he had it at home, come pick it up.

A friend named Lisk rode with me for the pickup. We

were due back at college for a banquet that night; we had to move. But when I ran downstairs with the suit on a hanger, Father's face dropped—Mother was out shopping. I at once knew the problem but tried to skate past it. I said "I'll come back this weekend and model it then."

Father stood and, with a brand new seriousness, said to Lisk "You'd think a fellow might get a glimpse of the suit he's worked to hang on his only son."

Lisk said a nervous "Yes sir."

And I said something about rush traffic.

We left and, halfway to college, Lisk said "You feel like a goddamned heel, I know." He'd lost his own father in the Second War.

I said "Not really. I'll see him, like I said." But we knew I was lying. And before a month could bring me home again, my father had been struck down and was dying.

And here tonight I'd howled in baboon glee at another kind elder who had meant me well. It's a not untypical quandary of youth, but I still don't think I was being sentimental. Even then I knew the difference between smiling at Chief's unworldliness and branding him an idiot and buffoon as we just had. I was deeply ashamed and knew I wouldn't sleep. I'd lie in the sound of seven sleeping boys and torture myself. But I was sane enough to realize that I couldn't go down now and wake Chief up, explain my guilt and beg his pardon. Lord, was he locked in Mrs. Chief's arms, cherishing the gleam he'd brought to her eyes?

No, I went to Cabin 16 and checked on the boys. With my flashlight I checked individual faces. All were out cold in various postures, all adding the din of confirmed mouth breathers to the peaceful night. I got my warmest sweater, my flashlight, a sketchbook and a box of colored pencils and headed back out.

A FAT NIGHT WATCHMAN NAMED CLAIBORN HAYES PAtrolled the grounds after midnight. He had every symptom of the abject pervert. One look and you'd easily have believed any mild charge against his stuffed white face—peeper, flasher, ladies' underwear thief, though he'd got through years with no complaint at Juniper. I thought for sure I'd run across him and need to explain. But otherwise I knew the place would be empty of all but me and raccoons, snakes, an occasional bobcat, owls, bats, a theoretically possible panther or bear and more than a hundred sleep-suspended souls, all known to me by face if not name—and all of them, trusting Bridge Boatner to spare their throats in the vulnerable dark.

Their trust was well placed, and I never came anywhere near seeing Claiborn. I've never since felt more soundly chastened for normal self-doubt. I knew I've never felt more well intended toward humankind. I went at first to the campfire ring. It was even darker there. I took up the flashlight to guide myself, then thought better of it and left things dark. I felt my careful way to ground level, the first row of benches, and settled in to say a few prayers. My prayers then were just people's names, as I said. But also by then I'd been so lucky I knew a lot of people worth naming. So the litany took maybe six minutes. Then I switched on the flashlight and tried to add to my angel sketchbook.

At that point in my work, I'd pared my art down to two things. There was a mainstream of more or less realistic pictures of places, things and people. And then there was a smaller branch of imaginary places peopled by creatures of the mind, my mind to be sure. All my life, not just since the recent encounter with death, I'd been fascinated by the fairly worldwide idea of angels. The English word comes from the Greek *angelos*, and *angelos* translates the Hebrew word for *messenger*. So an angel, in the sacred sense, is a messenger from and to a divine center.

Since for years I'd been sure that my work came from such a supremely powerful and knowing center, I'd taken to keeping a sketchbook devoted to it. In special moments, like tonight here alone, I'd try to set down quickly and with a minimum of forethought a guess at the face of an angelic messenger. Not that I really thought they have faces. I was making my own contribution to a line of glorious-to-silly guesses that stretch from at least the Ark of the Covenant down to those American primitives who even now portray the flaming message and the messenger through whom it reaches their minds and guides their hands.

I tried a Grecian-type profile, my usual first gambit. But nothing more would come. I clicked off the light and waited. Even in the night like this, I could only think of angels in color. Every color on any known prism. That was why, in dark thick as tar, I had my rainbow pencils in hand. In another black minute I imagined an eye, round as a marlin's, that blank but knowing. Then I opened the book and tried to draw it. It looked more like a doll's glass eye. I was too hemmed in—this circle, these close trees muffling me.

So I moved a short fifty yards to the lake, the far end of the pier. There I huddled down low and at once felt better. There was clear sky overhead, with stars so bright they were searing. Beyond was the distant splash of the falls off the mountain and the odd cavorting sleepless fish, whatever it knew. It was warmer here, with the deep lake holding yes-

terday's warmth. In a few more minutes, I switched on my
flashlight again and turned to my book. And in maybe five
minutes, I'd finished a face so filled with news, and all of
it good, that I thought at once I'd finished nothing better
since Father died. Again I doused the light, but the face still
burned before me. Its eyes were wider than human eyes.
Otherwise it looked like your finest friend, tuned to perfection in every cell. The lips were parted on the glowing coal
of news on its tongue, and a widening banner streamed
from the mouth. I meant that to be the meaning of life in
some angel dialect, not yet known to me.

Then I lay flat and watched the stars. I'd been an avid
consumer of popular astronomy since childhood. And for
years I thought of someday combining astronomy and art,
as a joint life's work. But then in high school, the hope went
smash on the reefs of algebra and geometry. I couldn't plot
the movement of a point on a line, much less the luminous
gears of the sky. Still from age eight on, I could find the
more famous constellations and some of the planets. So I
spent a few minutes now, scanning their light and specu-
lating grandly. Was anything new? Some new Child born?

And then I fell asleep, cold as it was. However long I
stayed unconscious, I had no sense of the chill or the
strangeness of where I was. I suppose I might very well
have stayed there till lifesaving class began at nine. Some
numb boy with his blue nuts cringing would find me, apparently dirty and dead.

BUT AFTER MAYBE TWENTY MINUTES, I FELT VIBRATIONS.
Footsteps were bearing down on the pier. It had to be Claiborn, the harmless deviant. Not that he'd care but my best
true alibi had to be sleep. I'd come out here with a case of

insomnia. The stars had worked their usual spell and I'd fallen asleep.

The steps reached my head, then stopped and stood. I heard the crack of knees bending and finally a voice that at first was strange. "You'll be dead in a minute."

I really was on the vague boundaries of sleep, so I didn't respond with words or acts.

And again the voice said "Mr. Boatner, sir, we got rules here. Don't go die on us." The vowel sounds in the word *die* lasted the better part of ten seconds—some Georgia cracker. Who but Rafe Noren?

I looked up and back and at first saw nothing, black empty space. Was I also hearing things? I sat up, stiff as a cripple, and looked again. And finally he appeared, a camper rambling alone in the night. Talk about rules!

I said "Is it morning?"

"Depends on your meaning. It's three A.M." Rafe stood a long moment, then dropped down a couple of yards away. "I'll tell you my secret if you'll tell me yours."

I accepted his deal. "You tell first though."

He said "I'm the only living child with insomnia. I lie down at lights-out with my whole cabin. Everybody tells jokes in the dark for a while. They try to talk sex, but they get it all wrong. And I don't know all that much more, to set them right, so I'm pretty bored. Then they slip on off, one by one. All but me." He seemed to be finished.

Again the strength of his voice surprised me, a firm baritone. All my boys were reedy sopranos. And the drawn-out vowels improved his effect. He could linger down low and, if you weren't looking, sound forty years old. So I tried to keep him talking. "What's got you awake?"

Rafe waited so long I thought he'd left. Then he said "You're bound to know."

"I do not, no sir."

He fumbled in his dungarees and found some object, which he hurled at the water. It made an earnest *thunk*.

I said "Was that your watch?"

He laughed a note, neither yes nor no. And then he said "I thought you counselors shared all your problem boys."

I said "Not always." Maybe I was still half asleep and dreaming. Anyhow I didn't feel urgently curious. I just didn't guess that Raphael Noren had a long hard story behind his eyes.

He said "Well, damn. I thought I was famous."

I told him he was—for dancing and wit, for general good sense.

Then his arm hurled again. But nothing hit the water. He said "You really don't know what I'm talking about, do you?"

I begged his pardon. "Honest to God. This is my first year."

Rafe laughed more fully. And that too deserved its local fame. The laugh was a joyful uphill rush, against his better wishes.

I thought we'd have half the camp down on us. But no light showed and nobody else came.

Eventually he said "I'm the richest boy in Georgia."

"Good," I said. "Put me in your will." If I hadn't known how unlikely it was, I'd have guessed he'd had a stiff drink or two.

He said "Let me get that absolutely right. I'm the richest boy in Georgia, *south* of Atlanta. They don't keep records for the rest of the state, the white-trash part. But I'm undisputed, statewide—let me tell you—for the sadness crown. Saddest boy, statewide. And if you know Georgia, that's a title worth having.''

I waited but, when he didn't say more, I sang two bars of ''Marching Through Georgia,'' with all its memories of Sherman's rampage from Atlanta to the sea, ninety years ago.

Rafe said ''Not that, more recent than that. See, my mother died four years ago. My dad's not home, always on the move, propagating our cash. Negroes raised me up, Negro men and women. Thank the Lord, I guess.'' It had come straight out of his mouth, slow and grave with no trace of self-pity. He might have been speaking to a bus tour of old folks, cruising the state.

I was way too tired and cold to disbelieve him, though I guessed I could hear the fascinated gaze of the born taleteller beneath his words. I'd check it with Kevin sometime tomorrow; he had Rafe's file. I said ''You know I ought to send you to bed.''

Rafe said ''You try it. All I'd do is torch your cabin, and you'd be responsible for seven fried boys—little barbecued white boys, all your fault.'' In that voice it sounded like a real possibility.

I said ''You're a lot too kind for that.''

The laugh again. ''You *don't* know me.''

So I asked to hear the rest of his record. Was it arson, manslaughter, first degree?

He said ''Calm yourself. You're planning to check my camp file, ain't you? Spare yourself the try—young Noren's records are sealed by law. Underage, don't you know?''

I said he was giving me the fantods now and he liked that. Then I asked how much he knew about sex. Sober though I was, and recently shamed, I was already hunting new people to regale with Chief's recent talk.

Rafe held off awhile. And then he coolly asked if I planned "to get funny"? If so, he'd wish me good luck in life and run like a dog.

I assured him *funny* was the last thing I was. And then because I was still feeling burdened, I went on and summarized the evening's events—Chief's talk, our laughter and my present regret.

Rafe Noren could listen as well as he talked. His face watched you keenly but with no flinch of judgment. For all you knew he planned any instant to hand you a wreath of deathless praise or lasting blame.

By then I was upright, leaning on a piling. The upper air was cold now, to taste of. I'd hoped to find such air all summer, a genuine surprise.

By the time I finished describing Chief's speech, Rafe had moved farther off still, three or four yards. But his watchfulness drilled through the dark between us. When I finished with what a worm I was for mocking the Chief, Rafe said "Chief well knows every bit of that, Bridge. Don't tell him a word."

"Of what?" I said.

"Chief knows that you all laugh at him. He's too good to care."

I asked how he knew.

Rafe said "He's told me. See, I've known Chief for countless ages, since before I was born. My dad came here in the 19-and-30s when this place didn't even have running water. They sent me up here when my mother died—two summers in a row, ten weeks every time. I tore the place up, I was so damned mad. Set a bonfire in the infirmary one night, smoked the nurse up bad and scared her even worse. So Chief decided to take direct charge. He moved me down to live in his house, just him and Mrs. Chief and that pitiful Clara. Clara lost about ten pounds, my first week there, just cold fear of me.

"And Mrs. Chief—Lord, bless her fat heart—called me aside and said 'Ray, we love you. Don't doubt that we do. But you got to live in the world that's *here*. Don't go try to ruin it. It'll just wreck you worse.' I knew she was right and told her so, and I meant to change. But the second week I threw a firecracker right in their commode—split the sucker in two! Chief didn't do a thing but politely ask me to step back in there and clean up the mess.

"It turned out I needed to mop the whole bathroom, about the size of the Everglades. Then he made me crawl up under the house, to see if water had got under the tile and soaked the subflooring. Talk about scared! It was darker than this whole night under there, and I wasn't more than ten years old. Seemed like the place for a snake *convention*. I found out the subfloor was bone dry though and the ground underneath. Then he let me come on back to daylight. Last summer I asked Chief why he made me do it, young as I was then and so fouled up. He just said 'Ray, nobody that can walk is too young to follow their deeds to the source.' " Towards the end of the sentence, Rafe switched to a voice that was almost identical to Chief's.

I said that sounded too tough to me, on too young a child. "But you said Chief knew about us laughing at him."

Rafe said "He mentioned that last summer too. Said something like 'Ray, do what you think is right and the whole damned world'll fall down laughing in the dirt. But pay it no mind—you plow right on.' "

"Chief said *damned*?"

Rafe said "I may have just thrown that in. I say it a lot. Makes me feel like an outlaw—*Dammit to Hell! Goddammit to Hell and you go with it!* And hell, it's about all the cussing a child can get away with."

I asked if somebody had been laughing at him, to provoke that strong a response from Chief.

Rafe said "Not but everybody, day and night. They laugh at my peculiar name, my dancing, my accent, my scary face."

"Where did your name come from?"

"My mother's favorite painter. I wish she'd liked somebody closer home—Winslow Homer or John Singer Sargent. Singer Noren *does* sound fine."

I debated telling him that Raphael was first and foremost the name of an archangel, but I wasn't sure I was ready to open that kettle of fish, so I just said Raphael was a perfectly good name. Then I asked "What's wrong with your face?"

He laughed. "I forgot you can't see in the dark like me. Cast your mind back to art class. Remember the monster that sits by himself and draws those simpleminded outlines?"

Long ago here I mentioned his premature manly look, so I thought he was angling for a compliment. I said "Poor lad, there's plastic surgery though. With his pa so rich, he can get fixed up when he's old enough."

Rafe waited so long that I suspected I'd again misjudged his age and endurance. I was about to say "Just kidding" when he said "I'm waiting till my looks come back in style, the year 3000."

Also in silence I realized he was right. They were otherworldly looks, swept back as if by a hot wind but strong enough to endure the blast. I said "Would you let me draw your picture?" He was the first human being I'd wanted to add to my messenger file. Not that he looked like a winsome cherub, at the edge of one of his Italian namesake's madonnas. He was just a credible Angel Gabriel, as Gabriel enters a real room ten-foot square and greets the girl rising to face him in the dim far corner, *"Hail Mary, full of grace!"* By that point I was ready to tell him. But without saying more I switched on the flashlight and showed him my sketchbook.

He turned every page, not saying a word, just little growls and grunts that seemed to indicate pleasure. After the first four or five pages, he got into the sexier angels.

I'd noticed that in Genesis 6 it says how the angels fell in love with some good-looking women. They came down to Earth and boarded the women. Nine months later here came children that grew up to be giants. William Blake had apparently noticed the same passage and illustrated it. So I was following Blake in drawing a few angels with enthusiastic genitals.

Rafe didn't especially linger over those pages but pushed on steadily through all. Then he handed me the book with nothing but "Thank you."

I waited a little, then asked if he thought they were foolish.

"I think they're the best thing I've seen since that albino deer."

I had to laugh. "When was that?"

"Hunting with Pa and his drunk friends. They were all out in their thousand-dollar hunting suits, shooting up the woods like World War III. I was about ten seconds away from giving it up and heading on home when, all of a sudden, here's a pure white doe. Just *there*, standing there, looking at us, not scared. Even the biggest jackasses shut up for a minute. And everybody watched like she was a ghost. I was pretty confused myself—I still think her eyes were brown, not pink. Whatever, anyhow I was speechless as a rock. I was storing her up in my mind for life. But one of Pa's friends fired a shot—the moron asshole of all south Georgia. Buckshot and broadside. Course he couldn't hit a fat chained-up elephant, thank Jesus. But I hit him, slapped his idiot face. Much to Pa's regret. When I got calmed down, the doe had naturally evaporated.''

The next step seemed as natural to me. I asked Rafe if I could draw him for my book.

"*Me?* Bridge, sir, you have got to be sick."

I played my ace. "Maybe you don't know but the Angel Raphael is one of the archangels in Hebrew tradition. And he's one that's specially well intended toward mankind. He enjoys talking to human beings."

Rafe laughed. "When did you cook that lie up, O Wise One?"

I told him it had been true, countless ages. *Countless ages* was one of his sayings.

He said he would check it in Chief's encyclopedia. He waited a good while to say "O.K. You got a secret place?"

"What's secret about it?"

Rafe waited. "I take all the guff I can handle, for dancing. Imagine if I was an angel too."

So with no great forethought, I said "We could walk up the mountain this afternoon, up back of the cabins."

"Your boys would follow us."

I said "You just climb up on your own. I'll meet you there by three o'clock."

Rafe said "And we miss Indian lore?"

I doubted that missing one day would ruin us.

Rafe thought and then suddenly said "God *damn*!"

I thought some nocturnal bug had stung him. "What bit you?"

He said "Not a thing but finally seeing the point. You're wanting me to pose for a live archangel?"

"That *is* the point."

Rafe said "Not my body, right?"

I said "Absolutely, nothing but your head. To tell the truth, it's your nose I'm after. You're the only living man in America now with a Grecian nose." He almost had one. His profile showed a perpendicular, barely curved line from the edge of the hair to the end of his nose. In the very rare cases when you see such a nose on anything but a classical sculpture, it can look unnerving.

Then Rafe stood up. "I got to get on."

I followed suit.

His good laugh broke loose again. "No, Bridge, you go lay your tired head down in Cabin 16 with all your little biddies. I got my rounds to make before light."

"Where you going, Rafe?"

"That's classified, sir."

"You do this every night?"

"Top secret, sir."

"Any girls out here in the woods, waiting for you?"

"I'm too old for boys' camp but not that old. Girls are a problem I'm saving for my next incarnation." He laughed, took a few steps and then said "You ever read *The Tibetan Book of the Dead*?"

This was fifteen years before hippies put that endless hodgepodge on the list of indispensable texts. I'd heard of it though, and the news that Rafe had read it was the knock-out punch for too full a night. I said "Don't tell me another word, son. I'll see you at breakfast." I was pleasantly tired and thoughtless halfway to the cabin. Then I missed my footing for an instant and nearly tumbled. As soon as I was balanced again, it dawned on me I'd made a real mistake. I should never have shown Rafe my messengers and asked to draw him. This boy was too nearly special already. He burned too high on too little fuel. I'd correct myself quietly in the art class at nine.

One thing I'd done right—going to the lake. Nearly blind, I'd managed to finish a good drawing. And I'd worn myself down so much that I slept through the bugle at seven. For the first and last time all summer, the boys woke me. When my eyes cracked open, seven boys were hopping in the cold at the head of my bunk, announcing at the top of their lungs that Bridge was lost in dreams of his sweetheart. I'd dreamed about her, more and more often, the longer I slept with these cool children. But the previous night she'd been as far from my dreams as her body was far. I quickly tried to recall who'd replaced her. Then I knew I'd slept past the reach of night visits. For all that I'd stayed up roaming till three, I was rested as a baby and honed for the day.

I WAS GOING TO NEED EVERY ATOM OF STRENGTH. THE morning went smoothly. Rafe didn't turn up for art class. But when I asked if anyone had seen him, one of his cabin mates said "He came to breakfast." I figured he was tucked in the woods somewhere or back in his cabin, sleeping off the night. I would just not show up for our meeting, and

Rafe would get the point—Bridge's new common-sense point.

WHEN I CHECKED BY KEVIN'S TABLE AT LUNCH, RAFE STILL wasn't there. Kevin said he hadn't been in his bunk at reveille, but that was fairly normal and Kev wasn't worried. Late in the hour's siesta though, one of my boys looked out the window by his lower bunk and said "Hey, Mr. B." The younger boys were in even more awe of Rafe's voice than his dancing. And they affectionately called him Mr. B after Billy Eckstine, the popular black baritone.

Rafe said "Hey yourself" and kept going.

I assumed he was making good on our arrangement, though he could have just been going to his cabin. For a while I considered going through with my plan not to show up. But a lifetime's inability to miss an appointment or to be a minute late eventually won. And when I broke out ten minutes later into the clearing where the boys and I cooked most of our cabin suppers, Rafe was sitting on the big rock. He was wearing a white T-shirt and his usual faded jeans—somehow he didn't like shorts. His right ankle was laid bare on his left knee, and he was studying the skin.

I could see at once that the ankle was badly swollen. I said "Tell me you haven't stepped on a snake."

He grinned and dropped his teeth. "Mr. Boatner, sir, I haven't stepped on a snake."

"What happened then?"

"Snake stepped on me, a timber rattler. Didn't see him till I felt this hot weight hanging on me. He was four foot long."

"God, Rafe. Where is he now?"

"I let him off easy. He's back in the woods."

I asked if he ever really saw him.

"Not only saw him. I was trying to pick him up."

It was one of those minutes when the world seemed *stopped*. There was no moving time, all clocks were dead. For once I knew not to start a lecture. I went straight to Rafe and inspected the ankle. There in nightmare perfection were two small puncture wounds. No sign of blood. In fact blood seemed to have left the whole ankle. For four or five inches around the punctures, the skin had flushed blue-white. And as I watched it, the swelling continued. Counselors were warned to carry rudimentary snakebite kits at all times. They looked useless but I always had mine—an alcohol wipe, a rubber tourniquet, a razor blade and a suction pump. I told myself *He's trapped in your plan, Bridge. Save this child.*

But when Rafe saw the kit, he laughed and said "Whoa, doctor. I don't want to bleed to death. Get me to Asheville soon as you can. If I pass out on you and don't make it, you take my headband." He was making a will in his head—that was plain.

I'd seen the headband. It was dark cowhide and Rafe had beaded it in white and blue, but that was the last thing I could think of now.

It turned out that, unlike many country boys, Rafe knew a lot about snakes. The general view, in rural America, is that you kill every snake you see on the off-chance it's poisonous. Rafe had taught himself to identify the few dangerous snakes of the South—moccasins, copperheads, rattlers and coral snakes. And he was way ahead of me in knowing that the latest medical thinking advised against the old cut and drain method, unless your cutter was an expert anatomist. Few snakebite victims die of the poison, but a good many wind up bleeding to death. You keep your victim as still as possible, which was why Rafe knew not to limp back to camp. Then you apply a tourniquet and carry him fast to the nearest supply of antivenin. Rafe also knew the precise brand of snake, a young timber rattler, apparently male.

His well-informed calm began spreading to me. I even had a moment to notice his face. He was pale, to be sure, and looked as if he might have lost fifteen pounds in the last few minutes. I'd brought along my camera, meaning to take at least a few photographs of his face for later use in my drawings. But unreal as he now looked, a camera was out of the question—the *human* question, that is. Naturally I longed to use it.

But I didn't. I laid my sketchbook and colored pencils under the shelving rock. Barring a hard rainstorm, they'd be safe. Then I said to Rafe "Stand on this rock. I'll tie off your ankle. Then you climb on my back, and I'll tote you downhill."

Rafe met my eyes and laughed. "Hey doc, you're doing all right." And he managed the two steps up onto the rock, but by then his upper lip was sweating, and his color was alarming.

I hurried to cinch the tourniquet. Then I backed up to him and said "Climb on." He put both arms around my neck and lay against me, surprisingly light. I hooked my arms beneath his knees and we started downhill.

I thought "I won't say a word about alibis. This child is too sick to worry about lies to save my skin."

But well before we hit civilization, Rafe said "Two things, Bridge. You heard me holler from up in the woods, so you came up to save me. And will you please ride to Asheville with me?"

I said I would if he needed me but that Kevin was the natural person to go.

He said "Kev's a gentleman but—see—I need you. You're my teacher and all."

I thought I'd want to think that through later. But I said, in that case, I'd square it with Kev. Then my own mind shut down, cold and scared. Another sick man was clinging to me. I felt my father's hot hand on my wrist. A human tourniquet, damming my blood. For a bad instant I thought *I can't*. But I didn't tell Rafe, and of course I obeyed him.

The rest of things fell out the right way from then on, that day anyhow. The first man I saw as we got into the camp was Sam, the head counselor. As stern-faced and upright as MacArthur at Corregidor, he'd been checking the showers for mildew.

I lowered Rafe to a bench in the shade, then called Sam over and described the crisis.

He studied the bite and said "Thank God you didn't try to drain it." He told Rafe how lucky he was I'd found him so quick. Then he looked to me, "The nurse has gone into town for supplies. She won't be back for an hour or so. You and I'll need to drive Rafe on in." He pulled out his keys and asked if I could bring Rafe a little farther?

Rafe got to his feet and looked around, entirely lost for his bearings.

I crouched to take him and we started the last few yards to Sam's car.

On the way we met the dietitian. Sam gave her the news in a dozen words and said "Tell Chief and Kevin Hawser. Kev's teaching his magic class in the lodge. Ask him to take care of Bridge's boys. Say we're fine so far and will phone from the hospital."

She put out a long efficient hand and touched Rafe's heel, just for five seconds but in tender slow motion. Then she met his eyes and said "Next week you won't know this happened."

My throat didn't lock but I said "Thank *you*." And that was the moment I understood how big a need any serious place has got for women. Women just always believe in a future.

But then Rafe tried to laugh again. It sounded old, that frail and high.

So from there on I was scared.

SAM DROVE LIKE THE OLD HERO HE WAS, FAST AND MASterly with an unhysterical but steady line of courage for Rafe and for me. While he must have known that snake lore was another specialty of Rafe's, Sam also gave us a lecture on the local varieties. How awful they looked but how seldom their bite really harmed a normal person.

I didn't look at Rafe, but I knew how far from normal he felt.

And by the time we got to the outskirts of Asheville, Rafe was needing Sam's courage even more than I. He was whiter still and beginning to shake, and his jokes had signed off miles ago.

For some invisible reason every car we met yielded right of way. We stopped only once, while Rafe leaned out to vomit in the weeds. And thirty-five minutes after leaving Juniper, we were in the emergency room, watching the boy be rolled away. He was all but transparent by then.

NOT TILL HE WAS OUT OF SIGHT DID SAM ASK ME FOR DEtails. I told him Rafe's lie. I'd heard a boy calling and thought it was Rafe. So I climbed the two hundred yards uphill and found him calm but already bit. As the words came out, I found I believed them. They sounded truer than the actual facts. Now if Rafe just lived.

Sam nodded and squeezed my shoulder. "You did fine, Bridge. He'll be all right."

If the story had been any less watertight, I'd have despised his gullibility. But as it was, I also nodded.

And Sam went on "Of course Ray should have been resting in his cabin after lunch, but he'll never march to any drum but his own. Not till life hits him harder than it has." Sam looked in my eyes. Then when I was silent, he kept on looking, "Christ knows, life's *tried* to down that boy— maybe you noticed. He's a likable boy but he draws hard luck."

I said I'd heard his mother died.

"Some years ago."

Sam was watching me still, and that was stirring my guilt to the boil.

But at last he forestalled me. "Ray still hasn't told you?"

"About what, Sam?"

"His mother, all that—"

I said "Just that she died when he was maybe ten. I've got the feeling he barely remembers."

Sam said "He remembers every second, Bridge. She was murdered, in Ray's presence." He went on slowly to tell a story as awful as any I'd heard to that point. Back then only four or five years ago, the Norens lived in the family's plantation house in south Georgia out in the open country. Ray was in the house one August day with his mother and a Negro maid. In the middle of everybody's afternoon naps, two escaped convicts walked in. Both of them were white, and one was a man that Ray's dad had fired some years before. They both arrived with homemade knives and at once tied Rafe up hand and foot, then his mother and the maid. They forced all three of them to huddle in a bathroom.

Then they ransacked the house for Mr. Noren's safe. The one fired man thought he recalled that the boss kept a safe. Finally they found it in a closet upstairs, but they couldn't break it open. By then they'd found a fine pair of pistols and tried to shoot the lock off—no luck either. Then they came back downstairs, yelling wild threats, and asked Mrs. Noren for the combination. She said she never had known nor had Ray. So they raped the mother and the maid right there, then cut their throats. They were starting on Ray when his father drove up with a truckload of fieldhands.

I must have turned pale myself by then.

Sam stopped and asked if I was all right.

I said maybe he'd better let up a minute; it had been quite a day. Then I stepped outside for some air. And hot as it was, with a few deep breaths, I pulled up short of passing out. But I thought of two questions and went back to ask them. Did Sam know the date of the day in August? Could yesterday have been the anniversary? He didn't know and, even up to now, I've never found out. I also asked if Rafe really witnessed the rapes and murders, and was he wounded before help arrived?

Sam said he'd always heard that Ray really was there in the room through it all but that—despite some blows to the head, when he tried to help the women—no, he didn't get hurt. Not his actual body.

Small mercy. I sat there this soon again in a hospital waiting room. It was the kind of place that had surrounded me through so many recent ordeals. Back then they all compounded the hardness of waiting with their milky green refusal of color and of all human sound but muffled grief or the slow unwrapping of one more cough drop. Even this late in a gangster century, a story like Rafe's is hard to take. In the gentle fifties, it was hard as downing a cup of hot acid. But down it went. I said to myself over and over the one thing I seemed to know, *I will not stay around for a life like this.* Young as I was, I put God, Time and Fate on notice.

THEY SEEMED TO RELENT. IN ANOTHER HALF HOUR A MEDical resident named Dr. Doak came out and said that Rafe was stable. It appeared he didn't get a full bite, not a full slug of venom. Maybe he'd lucked on an old snake or one that had flushed its poison sacs, hunting earlier today.

I felt it was important to say "No, Rafe specifically said it was young."

The doctor surveyed me as if I'd just clamored for classification as a maniac. Then he smiled faintly and said "Maybe young Ray's biological powers were diminished at the time."

I lamely said "Not likely."

Vindicated, he turned to Sam. Did Sam know of any past conditions—like rheumatic fever, asthma or seizures—that he should hear about?

Sam looked to me.

I said "No, nothing."

And Sam agreed. Apparently witnessing your mother's torture, rape and murder—and a family friend's beside her—didn't qualify. Sam added that Ray was strong as a bear.

Dr. Doak laughed. "A *talking* bear. That kid has told us

more, and about more things, in less time than any three other patients. But he's slowing down now.'' Then the doctor said that he'd like to observe Rafe for at least twenty-four hours, maybe longer. If there were no complications overnight, he saw no reason why Rafe shouldn't return to camp late tomorrow, provided we kept his activities light. But let's wait and see.

I knew at once what I owed the boy. I should stay nearby. But I also had seven boys back at camp, so I didn't speak up.

Sam read my mind. He looked to the doctor and said "Could Bridge stay here with Ray?"

Doak said sure, they were not too crowded and were putting the kid in a single room. They might even find a cot for me.

I wanted to say that *kid* was the last word Rafe deserved. But I looked to Sam and waited, as neutral as possible.

At once Sam said "If you'll help me out here, I'll personally sleep in your cabin tonight. You call me tomorrow if you need a ride back. Meanwhile I'll give Ray's dad a call.''

"You think he'll fly up?" Rafe had mentioned that his father owned a plane.

"Most unlikely, no. He's just remarried, for the second or third time. He'll authorize me to spend big bucks, buying Ray a toy. Let's go up now and see what he wants.''

WHAT THE DOCTOR HADN'T SAID WAS, RAFE WAS IN PAIN. The boy had never mentioned it, piggyback with me or in Sam's car. But once they got him drugged and in bed, he was free to complain. As we walked in his door, he gave a long moan. We must have looked shocked because the nurse turned, took a look at our faces and said "He's just playing possum. He's *pickled* in morphine."

Rafe said "The hell you say. That was saline solution—I read the damned label."

Sam laughed but said "Young man, hold your tongue. You know Chief and Mrs. Chief will be here tonight, so practice your cleanest company manners."

Rafe took it like a tired child, suddenly meek. He searched Sam's eyes and said "Am I dead?"

Sam was stunned for a moment and looked back to me.

I said "You're alive but with very little brain, just a few odd cells."

Rafe turned from me and searched Sam's face. "I asked you for the truth, Uncle Sam—don't fail me. What's old Ray's chances?"

It hadn't dawned on me that Rafe might be scared. But now I realized how hard he'd worked to spare me guilt and the chance of losing my job.

Sam said "Bridge was kidding. You're strong as an ox."

When he stopped at that, I took a step forward. "You're home free, Rafe. But the doctor wants you to spend a night, two nights at the most. Sam has asked me to keep you company. You mind?"

Rafe turned that over slowly. Before he looked back at me, he said "Sam, is that the plan?"

Sam said "I don't think it qualifies as a plan. I just thought it sounded like a good idea."

Rafe nodded. "All right." And then he faced me gravely. "You saved my damned life; might as well watch it awhile."

I smiled and said "Snakebite's not the terror it used to be."

Rafe wouldn't leave it there but shook his head slowly.

"I'll let you get bit next time then. Doctor said you got me here just in time."

Sam said "That's not quite what he told us, Ray. But we'll take any credit you want to hand out."

Rafe said "I'm talking to young Bridge Boatner. He got me down off of that mountain like a greased bobsled."

I said "I was scared."

Rafe said "*I* was scared—it was my damned bloodstream. You were the one stayed calm as a brick." His eyelids were heavy and his words were slurring. The morphine, or whatever the nurse had given him, was taking hold.

Sam said "Anything you need, big boy? Any Santa Claus letter you want me to mail?"

Rafe said "You been talking to my old man again?"

Sam said "Not yet but I'll need to."

Rafe said "Christ Jesus, omit that." Never again, in this world at least, have I heard that young a boy move the English language with that much assurance. Today every preschool child in the country can curse like a stoker. But what I mean is power with words, real bravery with words. Maybe in Rafe it came from the certain fact that he had got very few prayers answered, so he kept turning up the volume. In force, not loudness. I never heard him so much as raise his voice. The stronger he felt, the deeper it plumbed the lower octaves.

Sam laughed again and gave Rafe a hug that the boy accepted, with nearly full eyes. Then he eased out the door as Rafe drifted back on his pillow to doze.

I followed Sam into the hall. And all I remember from there is a long look at my eyes again and one question. "You sure you're up for this?"

I asked why I wouldn't be?

Sam said "I realize I hit you pretty hard with the news of Ray's past. I assumed you knew. It's built into all of us old-timers' hearts." For an ex-marine to confess to a heart was only the smallest surprise of the day.

I assured Sam I was fine and that we'd expect the Chiefs tonight. I promised I'd phone him tomorrow when we knew our timing. Then I gave him a few details on my boys—Darryl's bedtime insulin, Frederick's calcium, the full-length rosary that Barry's mother expected from him.

WHEN I GOT BACK TO RAFE, HE WAS STILL ASLEEP AND stayed so, right on till supper. He moaned occasionally and sweated a lot. Once when he was still asleep, he scratched at his arm and managed to paw his intravenous glucose out. You recall that was one of my nightmare memories of Father, tearing at himself. But I stayed cool enough and called a nurse.

She taped it back in and whispered to me "He's got to be in a world of pain. They always are when a rattler's involved, but he seems real brave."

That helped me notice her. Her voice was local, that high and raw. But she had a strong face, with fine broad bones, though again her green eyes were mountaineer eyes—laid back and cautious. I told her "He's been through a lot worse than snakebite."

She studied me quickly. "You his daddy, are you?"

I understood mountain boys started life early, but I had to laugh. "Sure, my oldest boy. I had him when I was seven."

She blushed a kind of terminal red. It didn't seem likely

her face would ever get back to normal again. Then she said "All right, *be* sarcastic then. You must be tired."

For the first time I knew how right she was. It made her looks and body all the better, her draw all the stronger. I'd had less than four hours' sleep last night and now all this excitement with Rafe. But here she stood, an obvious godsend. I had no idea what to say, only that I hoped I'd be near her for as much of this night as we could manage. Beyond that, I didn't think of ways or means. So I finally said "You working all night?"

At first she frowned as if I'd offended some law of kindness.

I put my hand up, outward in the air. I said I was sorry. "Please tell me your name."

She touched a small nametag I hadn't noticed and then came two steps closer towards me. It said *Tess Vance*—the woods up here were swarming with Vances.

But I didn't say that. I raised a finger to brush at the name.

She retracted a step and shook her head gently, just two slight sideways shakes. No, no. When I took her suggestion, she said "Doctor says you want to stay over. You can sleep right here, in that armchair. Or he says you can use the intern's closet. There's an army cot in there at least, and the intern's gone to Statesville tonight for his sweetheart's funeral."

"Lord, what killed her?"

As if I'd asked the day's dumbest question, Tess said "Well, love." Then she narrowed her green eyes and made a fine look of absolute mystery, *Now believe what I said.*

So I left it there—one doctor's girlfriend dead for love. And I said "How about me bringing the cot in here?"

She hadn't thought of that, and I saw how hard it was to thread a new thought through her rule-obeying brain. Finally she said "If you were his daddy—"

"All right. Say I am."

"But you're not. You just told me. You were seven years old when he—"

I whispered the clincher. "This child watched his mother raped and murdered. Now you're telling me I can't lie down here and guard him tonight?" Everything in her face made me want to withdraw my question and try again to love her tonight.

But she suddenly took both steps back towards me, and her face was lit with a new strong force. "You swear what you just said is the truth?"

I raised my right palm.

"You know it's safe here. We got night watchmen."

I said "It was safe at his homeplace too."

She said "Come get this old cot then."

WHEN I BROUGHT IT BACK, RAFE'S EYES WERE OPEN. THE nurse had said I could crank up the head of his bed, and now he asked me to do it. When he was nearly upright, he said "Please shut the damned door a minute." Once I obeyed he beckoned me close. Then looking past me, he said "Did Sam tell you?"

"You overheard me talking to the nurse?"

"I asked if Sam told you?"

I nodded. "This afternoon, while they worked on you." Rafe said "It's not all true. Don't repeat that story."

I told him I was sorry. "I just told the nurse what Sam told me." At once I suspected the obvious. Rafe had manufactured a three-ring horror show from lesser events.

But then he went on. "Sam's got it wrong. Chief and Mrs. Chief are the ones that know."

"You want to tell me?"

Rafe waited, then faced me one more time. "I do not, sir."

"All right. I understand."

With a sudden credible innocence that was hard to watch, he kept on. "You couldn't understand if you tried forever. But if you don't *believe* me, I'll just need to go back through everything. And see, I'm busy in here now—in my head—fighting off this timber rattler. Talk about the fantods."

I moved towards him fast and reached out to hold him. But he waved me back.

So I said "I believe you, now and for good."

That seemed to start easing him. His face slowly cleared and again I moved to show my affection. But in his most courteous voice he said "Bridge, please. I like you all right. I like what you do. You're a genius of the ages. But what I saw that day at home was a whole lot worse than what Sam told you. So please let's rest."

For the second time in the past ten minutes, I raised my hand to pledge my word. "I'll shut my mouth."

Rafe shut his eyes. "Thank you." Then his face went white again; his lips clenched down. The pain poured up him from ankle to eyes, plain to see as a rat in milk.

I said "Can I get you anything?"

"Not a thing on Earth, thank you very much." From some storehouse way beyond my reach, Rafe reeled up a grin. Then he dropped his front teeth. "Oh get my damned supper, Bridge. It's way past time."

I knew this child was far past me, in most known ways

and some unknown. And I knew it was the last thing he'd
ever let me say.

WE WATCHED TELEVISION TILL WE HEARD CHIEF'S VOICE
at the nurses' desk. Then Rafe gave orders like a four-star
general—cut off the TV, fix his hair, fix mine, was his
whacker hanging out? I managed to straighten up the room
in time. And when Chief walked in, we were combed and
cool.

Rafe said "Where's the madam?"

Chief said "I knew it; you'd just want her. Son, she sent
her deep regrets. But she's got a summer cold and didn't
want to share it."

Rafe said "You tell her she's got one last chance—make
me a lemon pie when I'm back. Just for me, not you. Or
else my good graces are *closed*."

Chief laughed and said he was sure he could promise that
much for her and no doubt a good deal more. Then he said
two amazing things, unabashed in my presence. He told
Rafe "You know how I love you."

Rafe said "Yes I do."

Next Chief turned to me. "We're all unspeakably grateful
to you, Bridge Boatner." He used both names, as if he were
reading a parchment scroll that preserved my valor for ages
to see. He'd also thoughtfully brought my shaving kit from
Cabin 16.

I mumbled a deeply uneasy thanks for the undeserved
praise, and I asked him to sit. I thought he might like some
time with Rafe, so I said I'd go down and get a breath of
air.

* * *

THERE WAS A FLAGSTONE TERRACE THAT OPENED OFF THE BACK of the lobby, and I sat out there. The long summer sunset was almost finished, and three lightning bugs had already struck up business in the unmown grass. The skyline was nothing too special, no pregnant sentence from the distant rocks but a nice line of trees that looked as ready as me for night and rest. When I first sat down, I was edgy. Wouldn't loneliness be a bad idea, after a day like this? Wouldn't I just start in on myself, with my old mental whips? Wouldn't my father rise again and say something hard?

To forestall trouble, for the first time in years, I tried to recite all the poems I knew. I was from the last American generation that memorized poems in school, and by now I had dozens. How many could I find? I dived in at random with John Masefield's "I must go down to the seas again." I moved on to Rupert Brooke's sonnet that predicts his own death, then Field's "The Gingham Dog and the Calico Cat," Tennyson's "Tithonus," Emerson's "The Rhodora," extensive selections from "The Rime of the Ancient Mariner" and every line of "Jabberwocky."

I thumped the varied rhythms on my thigh; and each one came out effortlessly, as if it was more than ready to serve. Maybe I was calling up the peaceful childhood I learned them in. Maybe it was just the comforting beat of meter and rhyme, like a mother dog's heartbeat among her blind puppies. But after I'd run through all I could find, I was empty as an upturned pitcher and as calm. And stars were taking over the sky, the mountain stars that shine so bright you think they're photographing you for your permanent record—*Watch it, son.* We're *watching you.*

A voice behind me said "Mr. Bridge?"

I looked and there was Tess Vance, Rafe's nurse. Her forehead was tense and that much scared me. She said "I think you'll want to come back."

I stood up quickly. "What's happened?"

Her face stayed worried but she said "Not nothing." Then she corrected herself, "Ray's company's gone and he's up there alone. I figure you don't want to leave him that way."

I thanked her and said she was kind to come down.

Tess nodded. "I know. I could get fired and worse, so I'm going to run. You come when you can." Then her white stockings moved. And her whole self vanished, like one more burnt-out lightning bug in the harmless evening which somewhere, somehow would see harm done to countless thousands, at home and abroad.

I'D STAYED HALF AN HOUR. AND WHEN I GOT BACK, I thought Rafe was sleeping. I couldn't be sure when the boy was really out.

But after a while, from what seemed sleep, he said "Try *not* to" with quiet force. A moment later his eyes were on me, though I seemed a rank stranger for twenty-odd seconds. At last he knew me and said "You don't have to feel bad, lying for us. We were doing good up there, meeting like we planned to. And this way we got a whole night and day to talk. You can draw me six ways to Sunday and back— angel, demon, dancer or dumbo. Get your pad out, doctor."

I told him, whatever he felt like now, I was worn to a frazzle.

He said "Not me. I mean to stand up." He threw back the cover and thrust out his legs.

"Rafe, stay put. Your ticker's had a full day, like it or

not. Your kidneys are filtering poison still. Calm down now and show yourself mercy."

"Nobody else has," he said. "Who am I to start a trend?"

"For that very reason," I said. "You can start a whole mass movement here tonight, mercy to Noren. You might even last to be a grown man. It's fun up here in the manhood zone."

Again Rafe studied me with the uncanny attention of a creature dropped in from Arcturus, and not necessarily benevolent. Slowly though he changed his mind and stayed put. He even smoothed the covers with meticulous care.

Thinking back I can realize that was the moment when Raphael, unarmed as he was, began to seem dangerous to me. Not so much a threat to my health as to overall life in the civilized world, which of course he was not. Maybe I really meant *endangered*. Like everybody else upright above ground, Rafe was in steady danger. At the same time even with him as weak as he was, I still thought of him as skilled and powerful, way past his years.

Sam's story, whether it was accurate or an underestimate, only added to the size of my error. This was a boy who had someway managed to use an event that was dreadful on any scale, and that happened in his home, to build himself a man's mind and body. I quickly recalled myself at fourteen. I was smothering then in alternate gags of self-love and -hate, sexual claustrophobia and dreams of obscene private power.

BY THEN IT WAS WELL PAST NINE P.M. THE DOCTOR STOPPED by to check again. He confirmed a continued improvement in Rafe's condition. Then he asked me to step out into the hall. There he repeated the fact that things were going nicely. The latest urinalysis had showed a decrease in the broken-down proteins from crotalid venom—the timber rattler is aptly called *Crotalus horridus*.

The moment I returned Rafe shook me down for every detail.

I saw that again he was genuinely presuming the worst, and I gave him another fatherly talk. I vowed that nobody was condescending to him by holding back bad news; there just wasn't any. He was coming along exactly as expected. If anything, better.

I did keep one thing under my hat—the doctor had said he'd been wrong in hoping Rafe could leave tomorrow. They really should watch him another day. I was going to let the doctor himself break that news when the time came.

Once I finished, a whole new calm moved over Rafe. Whether he decided to believe me, for some new credibility I'd earned, or whether he just had to fling himself on hope like a net, from then on that night, Rafe was like his best self, the one that danced and drew hard outlines—that steady and clear. We watched a little more dumb television. Then at ten o'clock he said "I wish you'd draw my picture now. That nurse you like, she'll give you supplies. A hospital's bound to have pencil and paper."

I laughed. "That nurse I *like*?—ah you're sharp, young Noren, but not sharp enough. We're *engaged* in fact. No, I think I'll postpone the art. You're no fit subject, tonight at least—a snakebit lad on the edge of exhaustion. Your angelic debut is yet to be. We're both turning in. Maybe tomorrow it'll be light enough in here for me to take some photographs." My camera was still with me, from our miscarried meeting at Juniper.

Rafe said "I don't pose for photos."

"Fully clothed," I said.

"I told you no."

I asked if he wanted to say why.

He seemed to plan it slowly. Then it came out as one of his more characteristic pieces of logic. "Most people in photos, at our house, are dead."

I left it there and stepped out to tell Tess Vance that I was ready to unfold my cot. She was nowhere in sight, so I told the head nurse. Did she have any last things to do for Rafe Noren?

She looked me over with standard medical disdain—from what bog of ignorance had I dared to crawl? Then she said "When I need to see the patient, I will."

I had the nerve at that point to ask if she knew the Latin word that *patient* comes from.

"No," she said, "but I bet Mr. College is going to tell me." This to be sure was back before everybody went to college.

I said "Yes he is. The word is *patiens*. And all it means is *sufferer*."

TO THE BEST OF MY KNOWLEDGE THOUGH, RAFE AND I slept more or less undisturbed. At some point in the darkness he woke me up and said "Turn off the loudspeaker, doctor. You're yelling too loud."

It was news to me and I denied it.

But Rafe said "Sorry, I heard every word."

"Then tell me."

"No sir," he said, "you'd never forgive me."

And I was back under, gone again. Later though I woke myself up at the end of what was surely a shout. I'd dreamed

I was deep asleep in a room with my father. He needed me and I couldn't move. Still in the dream I thought if I yelled loud enough I'd wake myself up and be able to help him. I thought I was yelling my actual name, but once I woke up, I listened for Rafe's complaint. He sounded asleep. So I got up to pee. I didn't turn on a light, and I kept as quiet as possible.

But once I was back and lying down, Rafe said "Don't let anybody ever tell you that you don't sleep like a damned baby—you do."

I wondered how a *damned* baby slept, but I said "How do you know? You're over there snoring like a sawmill."

He said it like a fact in court. "I have not shut an eye this night."

People in general won't let you cast aspersions on their sleeping habits, but I hadn't really heard him. For all I knew he was telling the truth, so I said he should have asked for a sleeping pill.

He said they didn't give sleeping pills to children and that anyhow it was normal for him. He didn't need sleep, just some quiet time to think.

I said "Is there anything you want to think out loud about?"

"And give you a quicky psychiatrist's license? Dream on, Bridge. Your guardian's awake."

I'm glad I remember thanking him. I also asked "Was I yelling my name just now?"

Rafe said "No, you were saying 'I'm sorry.' "

"Why didn't you wake me?"

Rafe laughed. "I figured you ought to be sorry, poor fool."

I laughed too, thinking he recalled Chief's sex speech and

the "pure tool." Since I was awake by then, I thought he might want to talk. So again I brought up the subject of his future. I guess I was so full of my own plans for life that I couldn't imagine a younger person not sharing my taste for the bright horizon. Would he keep on dancing or be a writer, since he read so much and used words well, or just a rich farmer?

Rafe said he lived "from sunrise to sunrise" and therefore didn't plan to lean on the future.

I gave him a short version of my sermon on the absolute duty that's on us to use any talent with which we're endowed by fate or whomever.

He was quiet till I thought he was finally asleep. Then he said "You talk about that tomorrow, Bridge, when your mind's a little clearer. Your tendency to babble has taken over. Remember what I told you. I'm on guard here. You're all I've got so my attention's undivided. Now go on to sleep. Christ Jesus in the sky!—you need rest, boy."

I gladly acknowledged that surely I did, but I told Rafe not to strain his back and eyes.

He said "Simmer down, boy. You earned you some rest."

Strange as it sounds I lay in that dark—hospital dark is as deep as dark gets—and thought *That's the thing I've waited to hear since spring. Somebody's awake so I can rest.* I recalled my unfinished canvas. I could see every misjudged stroke on its surface. Remember that, for a painter, the image a viewer sees is only one of thousands of pictures that lie stacked and smothered beneath the final abandoned top visible layer. Many times you long to recover a shape that you've now obscured, a whole idea that you think you remember. But you can't. *Press on.*

Under past conditions I'd have got up then, dressed and

walked back to camp to paint. But the sound of Rafe's breathing, plainly awake, eased me again. There where I couldn't see his size and youth, he did seem a thoroughly trustworthy watchman. And I knew he meant his pledge of care. So I lay back still and let my mind take a long free leap. I really do believe I fell down deeper than on any other night since Father's illness alerted my mind.

WHEN THE DOCTOR STOPPED BY RIGHT AFTER BREAKFAST, he told Rafe that things were clearing by the hour but that he should stay at least one more night. That would put everybody concerned "on the safe side."

Rafe just said "I can't speak for others, but the safe side's where I want to be, sir."

Once the doctor left, Rafe turned to me. "You thumb yourself on back to your job. I'll be all right."

In the next half hour I tested him from several angles and convinced myself that he was sincere. Then I checked with the doctor, who said "Go by all means. He's a strong little bear." So I gave explicit instructions to a nurse—Tess had left at dawn—to let us know if the least hitch developed. Then I asked Rafe again.

He said "Dr. Boatner, if you don't somehow get your nerves back into your *skin*, and then get yourself out of my sight, I'm liable to complain to the Youth Patrol and get your pitiful ass torn off." The Youth Patrol was a complicated and woefully incompetent paramilitary group he'd invented for his general protection.

SO JUST BEFORE ELEVEN THAT MORNING, I DID STEP OUT IN the road and *ventilate* my thumb, as we said back then in that last age of safe hitchhiking. Just that much time alone, with frank August sun pounding my head and clean mountain air rushing past me, felt like the grandest luxury yet in a lucky life. I was also thinking I'd won a round in my ongoing match with danger and death.

T H R E E

I'D BARELY BEEN MISSED. MY BOYS WERE DEEP INTO
rest time when I breezed in. Half of them were asleep,
but the others just looked up and smiled. One of them
did say "Boy, Sam is a lot stricter than you." And another
one asked about Mr. B—did he get to keep the dead snake's
skin? In spite of the tale of the Tsali boys' debacle, every
camper's heartfelt desire was still a snakeskin belt or hat-
band. But produce a real snake and you'd see all available
butts in unseemly flight. When I told my boys that Rafe's
snake was still loose on the mountain behind us, they got
respectful and dreamy again. They incidentally showed me
that Juniper campers had kept no tradition of Rafe's family
tragedy. Only the hard-core staff seemed to know, and that
was a real relief. I must have felt somehow that if Rafe's

own generation didn't know, then he stood a better chance of surfacing finally, alive and whole in a possible world.

First I climbed the mountain and retrieved my sketchbook, safe and dry. I kept my eye well peeled for the rattler but saw no trace. Then I hunted up Kevin, Sam and Chief and brought them up to date. Then I went to the Indian lore room. The boys there with Bright Day and Mike were much more concerned. How swollen up was he? Would his leg be well in time for the closing night dances? I set them straight and we all sat down to hear Day's little talk for the afternoon.

It was about the way various northern tribes would freeze a skin of ice on their straw baskets in winter and, that way, they'd have sealed containers for liquids and grains. We all nodded sagely, *Good idea*. Before anybody could press me harder, I ducked out, got my canvas and went to paint.

CONFRONTED WITH THE ACTUAL DISTANT SUBJECT, THE PICture so far looked as raw as I remembered. After one night away it seemed as unnerving as a flayed face. But I thought I understood my reaction. Rafe's near-miss made it all the more urgent for me to finish this painting. Finish it true and beautiful and—now—finish it in time for Rafe to see before he headed to Georgia.

Again I'm up against a serious problem here. The thing is, I need to describe my difficulties in painting a particular canvas without a boring amount of technical discussion or art-critic hot air and without reproductions of the picture in its various stages. The only writer I can think of who comes even close to managing the task is Virginia Woolf. Towards the end of *To the Lighthouse*, as Lily Briscoe the Sunday painter finishes her picture, I've always felt I can see the picture and taste its final success. It takes Woolf not much more than a page, but Lily's thrill in the quickening process shines right through. Strangely enough Woolf was not a painter, though her sister was; and they were close from early childhood.

Let me try this and then I'll drop it—my problem was limbs. How was I to interpret the space of eight miles that lay between my hand and the coded horizon, since that space contained no sizable objects to lend a scale? All eight miles were paved with leaves, hundreds of thousands of cubic tons of air and billions of green leaves and needles. And all of them were moving gently in the haze of opaque evergreen breath, which is what puts the smoke in Smoky.

A lot of good painters never learn to paint leaves. With help from Poussin and Constable and Gainsborough, I'd worked out early my solution for leaves. No, my problem now was to show what stood beneath the leaves and bore their immense weight towards me and the sky. I followed Cezanne and experimented on a smaller canvas with a system of planes that tried to hint at the bony struts under all that green. But a long look told me that tinted planes were just untrue. To my eyes anyhow, here and today.

What I wanted in the picture was the feeling I now had, watching this valley. Here was a whole bowl of splendid space made out of a few billion small green things. None of them broad as the palm of my hand. And under them all was the upward thrust of this powerful logical network of limbs. Once I knew that—especially once I got the notion of *logical*—a new courage seized me. And as if I'd learned it in my sleep last night, that courage showed me a code of my own, not just for leaves and the infinite spaces among them but, better still, the occasional ghost of a whole tree beneath them, right down to the roots. Patient and stronger than rocks themselves.

WHEN IT WAS ALMOST TIME TO QUIT AND GO UP TO CHECK my boys for cleanliness before supper, I'd conquered a palm-sized patch in the lower left quarter of the canvas. Right-handed painters tend to work from left to right. All around me boys and counselors were giving off the tired sounds of late afternoon. The words in the air were *shower* and *chicken*. It was fried-chicken night, which also entailed home-cranked ice cream. Even that sorely tempted, I could hardly stand to quit. And nothing but the coming of sunset made me. Otherwise I'd have let the boys find their own way to the feeding trough.

For the first time in my life, I had the sweet desperation of suspending fruitful work with nothing stronger than a prayer that I survive the night with mind and hands intact, such as they were. And to hell hereafter with any such hedging. I'm a serious artist now and I was then. I also knew it. In my experience the ones who always cry *'Umble, 'umble* turn out to be exactly that. Humble indeed, in power and stamina. In any case for the first and last time, I had another prayer. I said it directly through the air to Rafe Noren. It was bountiful thanks that his latest bad luck, which I'd partly caused, had now bloomed out in a beautiful usable thing that he could see and understand. As I'd seen his daring and learned my own.

I WOKE UP AT THE FIRST HINT OF DAWN, SLIPPED INTO MY shorts and ran downhill through the cold light for confirmation. Had it lasted the darkness? Was it as good a solution as I remembered? Even in the white early light, even when I took it to the Indian lore room and examined it there in the makeup mirror, I could honestly say a solid yes to both worries. So I sat on the nearly frozen terrace and worked for an hour till reveille. I galloped uphill and rushed my boys through wake-up and breakfast. Then I briskly posted my class to their several viewing stations, while I settled in to paint air and leaves and their unseen piers.

THAT KIND OF SEIZURE ADVERTISES ITSELF. WHEN I STOPPED by Bright Day's table at lunch to say I'd miss Indian lore again today, he said "All right." That was a voluble outburst for a man as careful with words as he. But then he laid a huge lean hand over mine, there flat on the table. And he said "The important thing is your *eyes*." With both forefingers he drew long lines in the air from his eyes. He'd seen the picture late that morning but hadn't said anything till now.

No white man to that point, and only a few dippy white women, had ever called my work visionary. But Day's word *eyes* sounded hard and at least half true. Secretly I took it as a license, and a license from people who knew a vision when they saw one. Bright Day was still for instance rehearsing his clutch of white doctors' and lawyers' crewcut sons in a bone-earnest Ghost Dance that meant to rewind our tragic history and redeem it with permanent peace. He knew I knew it, and he knew we'd agreed in mutual secret not to discuss the outrageous fact.

THERE WAS NO SIGN OF RAFE AT SUPPER. I WENT TO SAM'S table. He said the doctor had phoned and confirmed Rafe's progress but wanted to keep him just one more night. Sam added that he'd also spoken with Ray. "The boy surprised me. He sounded almost homesick for us. Asked about a painting you're doing. Sent you good luck.''

Since the doctor had told Sam to collect the boy anytime after breakfast tomorrow morning, I didn't worry. I only wanted to have as much as possible accomplished on the surface of my picture in time for his arrival. So I worked that night by electric lamp, a source I seldom use. In this case I felt endorsed by two things. The first was a need to show Rafe some reward for a trial that I'd at least triggered. Second was my firm memory of the colors of day in that valley between me and what those limbs and rocks were meaning.

TOWARDS MIDNIGHT I HEARD SOMEBODY IN THE HALL OF the crafts cabin. At first I thought it was Claiborn, the watchman. Then with a chill of surprise, I thought it might be Rafe, back and prowling the dark again. Fine. I was ready.

It was somebody else but welcome also, to me at that point. Bright Day suddenly stood in my door.

I realized I'd never seen him after dark. He slept in a small back room at Chief's. But did he go to sleep that early or work in his room? I must have expressed surprise to see him.

He waited to let that fly on past him. Then he said ''I want you to know now. The night before our council fire, you will be inducted into the tribe here. We leave it to you to make preparations with the Spirit in the way you choose.''

I'd heard from Mike Dorfman that there was such a tribe, consisting of staff and a very few campers. Induction was earned, not applied for; and the standards were secret. I assumed that the elders were Mike, Chief and Bright Day.

And I'd left it at that with a lingering suspicion that this was a strictly local mystery, something else that couldn't be safely exported beyond the gate of Juniper. A good deal that seemed dignified, even beautiful, here would surely seem laughable the day I left. So now I felt a certain shame-faced pleasure, an honorary brave in a nonexistent tribe at a rich white kids' camp. But to Bright Day then and there, solemn as if he were bringing the wing of a snow-white eagle to Crazy Horse in full moonlight, I bowed my head and said thanks.

Day said simply that I'd earned induction. Whether it was for my painting, my care of Rafe or what, he gave no hint and I didn't ask. Then he said I'd be told when and where to come on the night in question. Meanwhile stay silent. He turned to leave, took three steps, then looked back again. "You are free to refuse."

I shook my head and said I was honored.

Day waited in place, maybe giving me one last chance to refuse. Then he put a hushing finger to his lips and was finally gone.

It was a gauge of both Day's weighty tone and my own present mood that I suddenly wondered if he meant me to stay entirely still till the induction or just silent on this news. I rose to ask him—too late. When I got to the terrace, I saw a body swinging, pendulum slow, toward Chief's. But late as it was I didn't call.

And Day didn't look back.

AGAIN NEXT MORNING I WENT DOWN EARLY. TILL HERE and now more than thirty years later, the whole left half of the picture is veiled in a soft dawn light while the rest is frankly sprawled in sun. Knowing why, I've almost enjoyed the difference. And viewers seldom ask about it.

At breakfast nobody mentioned Rafe's return. Kevin and his boys were normally groggy with their oatmeal and stewed fruit. I didn't ask them. And Sam didn't stop by and ask me to ride with him to Asheville. So I met my class. For the first time I tried to apologize to them for possible neglect. Truthful or not, they all said they were learning more from watching me. To be strictly honest, they said they were having more fun this way. So I plunged back in.

Even at the time, I recalled a story from my history professor. When the great founder of the Jesuit order, Ignatius Loyola, was a student at the University of Paris, somebody asked him, while he was playing tennis, what he would do if they learned the world were to end in an hour. And Ignatius said "I'd go on playing tennis." Whatever my world was about to do, I went on painting my slice of the Smokies and felt a good deal more heroic than the facts called for. I was further elated by the wait for Rafe. Surely he'd be back in time for lunch.

Rafe Noren's return from what appeared to be an uncomplicated snakebite seemed one of the simpler rescues of his life. But my mind was not in simple condition, as I've tried to show. It was still hungover from my father's death and from all my grappling with unearthly codes and angel faces, not to mention the news of Rafe's old horror and the net of lies he and I had strung beneath us. So a boy's return had taken on unnerving size in my life that day.

I WORKED TILL LUNCHTIME BUT NEVER SAW RAFE OR EVEN Sam's car returning from town. When I got to the dining hall though, Rafe was at Kevin's table. The dietitian who'd promised him life was standing over him, rejoicing in her foresight. And Mrs. Chief was awaiting her chance. Rafe was standing by a chair, answering questions with his old self-possession—no fearful boy now. He was maybe a little peaked in the face. He certainly looked a pound or two lighter, and his tan was fading, but otherwise he looked very much like himself. Once my boys were served and bolting their food, I thought of stepping over to welcome him back.

But by then more boys had gathered round him, and I'd almost swear that one of them asked for his autograph. Anyhow Rafe wrote something brief on a napkin and handed it over, whatever it said. And the boy who got it ran out the screen door and on up the hill, abandoning lunch. Triumphant return from the jaws of death had only increased Rafe's power over other boys, and he didn't mind showing the site of his wound.

He did seem to avoid my eyes. I thought he was up to one of his jokes, so I didn't go over and inquire. I hung around a few minutes, talking to Mike Dorfman. I wanted to ask him confidentially about the silence Bright Day had mentioned.

Mike said "Nonsense"—a healthy lot of the world was nonsensical to Mike—and then assured me that Day had only meant not telling anybody else before my induction.

When I finished with that, Rafe still hadn't walked over. In fact he was gone. So I went on to Cabin 16 and put my boys on their honor to rest quietly. Then I went to the *Thunderbird* office to cut the last stencils for the final issue.

BY THE END OF REST TIME, I WAS A LITTLE EDGY ABOUT seeing Rafe at Indian lore. I'm a normally productive human guilt factory, and by then my production line was going into overdrive. This strangeness was somehow my fault. Still I went on to Day's workroom at two o'clock.

No sign of the boy.

Day talked about the subtleties of Amerindian sign language. Its hundreds of gestures had provided a rich medium of exchange between tribes who spoke incompatible tongues or dialects. He explained that it was one of the best-preserved of all the Indian achievements. And he suggested that—if only we'd haul it out and begin to teach it in the early grades of school—it would make an excellent medium for international understanding until such time as everyone agreed on Esperanto or whatever. Those to be sure were times when the United Nations was an actual force in the world, not just a dildo for the Third World.

When Day had finished and the time came to break up into small work groups, I managed to whisper a question to Day. Was there something I needed to make for my induction, like a headband or breechclout?

In his normal voice he said "Sunday clothes."

In that case, I told him, I'd go back to my painting now and finish the bonnet in a few days.

He nodded and then looked up past me. I noticed that his face had firmed with surprise. He waited a moment and then said "Should you be here?"

So I looked too.

Rafe had come in quietly and was sitting in a corner, beading his moccasins. He answered Day in almost a whisper "I can do anything that's peaceful."

I thought I'd walk over and ask for the doctor's final report.

Rafe didn't look up but continued "I'm all right, thank you, sir."

"Will you feel like dancing at the council fire?"

"I felt like dancing yesterday." He didn't seem hostile, just mildly drugged and businesslike.

I thought how often sickness did that, seized you out of your normal circle and skewed your pace. He'd be fine soon. So I told him I was glad and that I'd like to show him something if he'd come out to the terrace now.

He said "I will, directly." Back then *directly* was polite Old Southern for "Whenever I'm damned good and ready and not before."

I'd learned enough about the attention span of adolescent boys to hold my own in response to the chill. So I went outside and relaid my palette. In five minutes I was back in the only constantly peaceful world I know the way to. And I painted on through the full length of the afternoon classes. I was waiting for Rafe to see the picture now and stamp it with his good natural taste. Finally I heard the boys running away from Indian lore, howling like the Indian stereotype of white men—undignified yahoos. By then I was uneasy. I'd plainly offended Rafe.

At that moment I saw him aimed towards Chief's house, downhill from me. Apparently he meant to check with them, maybe to allay Mrs. Chief's worries or to collect his lemon pie.

I couldn't resist saying his full name in a natural voice.

He stopped and looked around but didn't wave or speak.

I asked if he would stop by on his way back.

I thought he nodded but again he didn't speak.

I went on working and, in maybe twenty minutes, Rafe climbed the hill and stood a good distance off.

I asked if he'd got a clean bill of health?

"From *them*, yeah. They know as much medicine as I know Turkish."

I told him, from the looks of things, he'd better take life easy for the rest of the week.

He said "If I take it any easier, my heart'll stop, doctor."

Now that I'd noted his contempt for M.Ds., I began to wonder what irony was concealed in this new nickname he'd laid on me as I was applying the tourniquet. But I said "Please cast an eye on this."

He hesitated, then walked around behind me and studied the canvas. He looked a good while and compared it time and again with the view. Finally and without looking up at me, he said "Raphael Noren thinks it's pretty damned splendid. That may not be what you need to hear."

I was genuinely pleased. I knew he could lie about daily facts. But when called on to express an opinion or a judgment, he told the plain truth as he saw it. What was this new truculence towards me though? For two days now I'd debated whether to give the picture to Mother or Viemme, but now I said "Would you like to take it home week after next?"

Rafe said "The whole picture?"

"With my thanks, yes sir."

He waited again. "Thanks for what? It's honor enough, just knowing you offered it. But Bridge, my life'll be so gypsy, I doubt I need to own big objects."

I laughed. "With that accent you'll stay in Georgia or never be able to order a meal in any other language or dialect of English."

Rafe had told me the true story of an old backwoods Georgia legislator who, in a debate on the compulsory requirement of a foreign language in state high schools, rose proudly and in a voice heavy with passion said "If the English language was good enough for my Lord and Savior Jesus Christ, it's good enough for me!" Rafe grinned at my joke and then made a series of gestures in the air, using both his hands.

It looked like a snatch of dance practice, so I said "What's that?"

"Amerindian sign language, doctor." He repeated the signs, with a running translation, "Dried venison—cherries—cornmeal mush."

I laughed. "You made it all up."

"Swear to God," he said and raised his right hand. "You go ask Day. You said I couldn't order a meal, outside of Georgia, but I just did." He rubbed his stomach and smiled again. "Anyhow you don't need to talk to be able to *run*."

I understood a new fact and offered it to him. "You're no runner, Rafe—I see that now. You're a stander, the man who stands and takes it."

He said "When I'm tied down, sure."

I'm glad to say I didn't have a quick reply. I painted a few more small strokes.

Then he said "Look, sir, I better get indoors. This sun is heavy and I'm getting woozy."

I reminded him there was a cot in the Indian lore room. But he said no, he'd head for his bunk.

At that point in my life, I still possessed the normal human appetite for rejection. I said "Last week you were pressing me hard for this picture. So I want you to have it."

Rafe was walking away. He barely slowed down but in

his lowest voice he said back towards me "Wantin' ain't gittin'—."

That struck me wrong. I said "Stop right there. How have I hurt you? All I did was neglect my own seven boys to watch over you. Remember why?—you asked me. When I left the hospital, both of us know you were already well. And remember too, you told me to leave. I had another job."

He smiled again. "Of course you did. Everybody that's ever left me had a real good reason. My mother had as good a reason as any dead human—a man cut her throat. I'm aiming at a life now with nobody in it."

I said "That's the saddest thing I've heard."

"When? Today? This year? Since your father's last words?"

I said "That's it. Rafe, I'm mad. And now I know what a damned baby is. Go on. You need sleep."

He made a slow bow, said "Amen, Lord" and walked away.

AND IN LEAVING OUR MUTUAL ANGER SUSPENDED, HE RE-minded me of one more useful home truth. You *work* your way through private trouble. To echo one of the many sports philosophers of the time—you tuck your chin, hug the ball and step high right on down to the goal. Or you'd damned well better learn how to try. That afternoon I worked right up till time to be sure the boys were combed for supper. The canvas was now half covered, half done. And though it had a new forlorn air, I trusted its own inner weather would clear when mine did. For now I'd had a bellyful of the ingrateful rich.

Both Hemingway and Fitzgerald were wrong in their no-

torious exchange on the subject. The really rich *are* different
from you and me—they're starved. And what they crave of
course is what we never give them. The way other people
want peace and quiet, the rich want absolute love and loy-
alty in *spite* of their money. If you don't believe me, then
don't ever try to feed one. You'll be chewed up, swallowed,
digested and flushed before you can cry "Help!"

THAT NIGHT'S EVENT IN THE LODGE DID MANAGE TO RAISE
the mood a notch. It was one more Juniper tradition that,
late in each session, the boys produced a stunt night. In an
odd loosing of the reins, Chief instructed us not to help or
curb them. This was their free night and anything went,
except blasphemy. So as always apparently, the boys planned
and rehearsed in gigglesome secrecy for days. The staff of
course expected to be roasted, to a turn. Rumors of years
past suggested that the unleashed boys would leave no one,
even the Chiefs, unsinged.

And they more than delivered on expectations. A description of each cabin's skit would soon be cold oatmeal. It's
enough to say that my boys put together an unnervingly
accurate parody of me, from accent and gait to gestures and
subject matter. I had to laugh good-naturedly, to be sure,
since every eye in the lodge was racing from stage to me
and back. But like all the lampooned always, I strained to
hide my initial shock. My boys had watched me a lot more
closely than I knew.

I was, one more time, the homely turtle torn from its
shell and exposed to the light. But I labored to seem both
flattered and amused. Once the Cabin 16 boys finished
though, I soon felt I could count my blessings. The boys
after all had homed in on my absorption in painting, nothing

worse. They'd even gone so far as to locate a genuine Parisian beret which "I" alternated with a full war bonnet as I slashed away at my easel. Otherwise there were no big revelations, except a glance at my awkward triumph in saving Rafe. At the end of the skit, their "Mr. Covered Bridge" loped offstage in the best Groucho manner with one of his "disciples" riding piggyback.

After several more kindly ribs—including a genuinely funny look at the Chiefs' square dancing—the night ended with Kevin's older boys, our hormone cases. They dramatized in a generally obscure way the teenaged sensation of the summer. Nobody but the perpetrators and Kev and I knew for sure that, the previous week, Kev had gone looking for three of his boys who didn't turn up for rest time. Just as he was about to give up the search, he glanced into the stable. All three boys were standing intent on the rails of a horse-stall door, engaging in successive congress with the camp's oldest and gentlest mare.

I'd have guessed that Rafe's three-day absence had removed him from action. But no, he took the part of "Blevin"—angrily hunting the truant boys, then finding them with wild aghastment. His gestures and voice again were prematurely expert. But his cabin mates had proceeded so gingerly, for fear of shocking the Chiefs, that they ended with a mystifying dud. It was funny to the few in the know but pointless to the rest.

My boys looked at me and made the current sign for *dumb*, a forefinger circling the air at ear level. And at the close there were even scattered boos.

As the older boys took their bow, I saw Rafe's face in genuine embarrassment—his first stage failure and in a hard week. I remember only a touch of surprise that he'd risked exposing Mrs. Chief to the secret.

OTHERWISE THE DOG DAYS BORED IN. EVEN IN THE MOUN-tains, noonday heat was a punishment. And an expectable monotony and exhaustion had begun to sap the boys. But the next evening after what seemed like a normal supper, the lights dimmed overhead. And the waiters brought in a tall white cake with a forest of candles. It turned out to be Chief's birthday; nobody said which. Even his pink lungs couldn't manage that many flames on a single breath, but he made it on three. Then to cheers from all, the waiters returned with smaller cakes for every table and bowls of strawberry ice cream.

Toward the end of eating, a few old campers began to chant "Dive, Chief! Dive!"

I looked to Kevin two tables away. He was as puzzled as I.

But Rafe turned to Kev and mouthed some message.

Kev passed it to me. "Chief always dives in the lake on his birthday, believe it or not!"

I couldn't, not at first.

But in ten more seconds, the chant had mounted to a genuine roar—even Rafe joined in.

With a sheepish grin Chief finally stood and moved to-wards the door. A crowd of boys rushed to join him; and of course the staff followed, amazed. The thought of Chief diving into Juniper's lake, which was maybe five degrees above freezing at noon, seemed way past belief.

WHEN KEVIN AND I GOT ONTO THE PIER, WE WERE JUST IN time to see Chief climb to the platform of the twelve-foot tower. As if he were shut in his own bedroom, he slowly removed his shirt and trousers, folding each carefully and handing it down to Mrs. Chief. Then he climbed the last steps and turned to face us. Under his clothes he was wearing a 1920s bathing suit, capacious woolen trunks and a moth-eaten tank top.

If he'd levitated up and away in the lovely evening, on past Camp Tsali and the prayer circle, I couldn't have been more astounded.

The same hush had spread to the boys. Their yelling and stamping was now tense awe.

Chief looked down to us, gave his split-second grin and his puppet wave, then spent a while gazing up. I assumed he was praying. God knows, I'd have prayed. Fit as he was, Chief had to be sixty or sixty-five. Then in four short steps, he was at the brink. To a general gasp he clamped his nose and fell onto space. His long white legs bicycled the air.

He took about a minute to hit the water, or so we all thought. Then he took another two minutes to surface and start a stiff crawl to the landing stairs.

My share in the general glee was mixed with a few grades of fear. Had he overreached? Would he climb out and die? Would we come down for breakfast tomorrow and find white lilies on the door of the dining hall? What I showed of course was the same wild praise that rang around us.

Then with no help at all from the forest of arms that reached out to raise him, Chief pulled himself up the ladder to the pier. He was soaked and pale and not smiling yet, but he seemed to be fine. Even his thin legs were firm as he stood and accepted a towel from Mrs. Chief. When he raised both clasped hands above his head and finally grinned, we all could barely believe our luck. He'd done it and was safe.

But most of the way uphill to Cabin 16, I was working hard to slow my heart.

As I turned in there, Kev passed with his boys. They were noisy still with Chief's new miracle.

And calm in their midst, Rafe grinned for the first full time in days. My back was turned but I heard his voice. "I'll love old Chief long after I'm gone."

If he hadn't put that final kink in his declaration, I might have forgot. But there it was.

AND THEN WE WERE DOWN TO THE LAST WEEK OF CAMP. Next Saturday the parents would redescend. The counselors would clean the place up and be free to go on Monday. All that of course meant the tribal induction ceremony on the next-to-last night and then a final campfire, with Day's Ghost Dance. No one had mentioned it again, but for me it also meant that I still owed myself and the Creator a visit to the prayer circle.

And that meant making a personal prayer stick to add as my token, a votive offering to what was apparently a small thicket of sticks already there. So I had two secrets to keep, the induction and Bright Day's laconic mention of spiritual preparations. Plus a bonnet to finish for the powwow, the final issue of *The Thunderbird* and a writing up of final evaluations to give each boy's parents as they hauled him away.

In all the work of that fifth week then, I hardly saw Rafe. Sam gave me a good report after he'd driven the boy in for one more check. But Rafe, he said, was lying low, taking extra rest and seeing the nurse every day after breakfast. I hadn't expected such self-control from a reckless child's mind. And it took a good deal of the edge off my push to finish the picture. With Rafe out of harm's way, my private solution to the meaning of things didn't seem as white-hot urgent as it had. Still the canvas was well within seeing distance of final completion. The bonnet was finished and hanging on a hook in the Indian lore room, and the prayer stick was underway.

I'D FOUND AN IDEAL PIECE OF WORMY CHESTNUT, THICK AS my thumb, dry and dense. I studied the knots and grain and worm holes and then sketched a design that involved a timber rattler coiled loosely up the stick towards the simple strong face of a boy at the top. My purpose was to offer thanks for Rafe's rescue and my part in it. Nobody but me knew how implicated I was in the boy's latest near-disaster. Even Rafe didn't know the full extent of my satisfaction in being able to do for him what I'd failed to do for my father.

So I worked on that job exclusively in Cabin 16. I told my boys it was a walking baton, like an officer's swagger stick. And they asked no probing questions about the primitive snake and boy. Just an occasional "Is that Ray's snake?" and I'd say "Yep." They must have assumed the head was me.

AS THE PAINTING REACHED CONCLUSION THOUGH, A SUD-den small fame spread through the camp. There was hardly a camper or staff member, down to the waiters, who didn't make at least one visit to the terrace where I continued working for a good part of each day. Some just watched in humming silence, but even the silent watchers would thank me before they left. And every spoken comment was good;

it was my introduction to aesthetic praise. The great Sargent said "A portrait is a picture with a little something wrong around the mouth." That summer I might have said "A realistic landscape is a painting your average citizen wants."

And one of the boys at Juniper explained the reason when he studied the picture and finally said "That's a place I'd really like to be." A smart aleck said "It's where you *are*, stupid." But the first boy said "No, it's safer." One of the boys from Texas asked the price. I underestimated, saying five hundred dollars. And he was ready to phone his father then and there and secure the sum from his trust fund. Several more said their fathers would buy it on Sunday. I had to say "No, this one's mine." In the face of Rafe's refusal, I'd made that decision.

On the Thursday night of that last week then, I went through a counselor's normal duties. In this case I helped my boys collect their various acquisitions for packing. Headdresses, lanyards, bracelets, pottery bookends, slingshots. I even had the previously unknown oddity of hearing one camper in quiet tears after taps. Five weeks were too short; he didn't want to go home. But after I'd lain on my bunk long enough to hear them all asleep, I got up and put on my dress whites. They consisted of a long-sleeved shirt, duck trousers, socks and white buck shoes. Since the night was normally cold, I wished for a white coat but had to fall back on a red lumber jacket. Then at a little past nine, I took the flashlight and headed for the campfire ring with no certain notion of what to expect.

On the walk over I was nearly swamped by a wave of embarrassment. Twenty-one years old and here I was, dressing up for induction into a nonexistent Indian tribe consisting almost entirely of white men and boys. What next?—membership in my local Moose Lodge? I actually stopped and stood thinking for a good thirty seconds.

This was something I could tell to Mother. But gentle as my girl Viemme was, I knew I'd better not run it past her. She'd laugh all night. I'd been thinking of Viemme more and more lately, mostly at night. After the one bad long-distance experience, I'd never tried again to phone her. In matters of the heart, I can shoulder my way past a lot of cheating, if I don't have to watch. But she and I had kept up a healthy blizzard of mail between Maine and the Smokies. My marginal drawings had got even warmer, and both of us claimed to be counting the days till we met again. I was sure we'd soon be reviewing our big postponement—not the question of marriage but a final Yes or No on the fuming issue of All-the-Way.

Suddenly Kevin was behind me in the dark. "You by any chance headed for this thing of Day's?"

I said "Just maybe."

Kev laughed. "I know. But we're *artistes*, Bridge. And this is life. Let's plunge and drink!"

WHEN WE GOT THERE, IT WAS PITCH DARK. I HEARD SOME whispers down in the ring itself, so we started walking towards them. I figured they'd stop us if we weren't wanted yet. My own dark rambles had taught me how to navigate here in utter night. So when Kev said "God, I'm blind at last," I said "Hang on." He stepped behind me, both hands on my shoulders; and I led him down like what he claimed to be. Nobody stopped us and when we got there, the voices were Mike, Bright Day, Sam and Chief. They seemed to be working on something in the dark. For an instant the air felt sinister to me. I remembered childhood well enough to know that people can change in the crack of a moment, from good to evil, with bloody teeth. Who were these men now, and were they still men? But with Kev behind me, we walked on down. When we whispered our names, what sounded like Day matter of factly asked us to sit on the first row of benches.

That was when I realized we were almost late. Roger the swimming counselor was already seated and waiting. So was Jim Todd, a senior boy who'd been at Juniper for six summers and was the one other camper besides Rafe who'd really studied Indian lore on his own at home. Nobody was using flashlights, but by then my eyes were more open to the dark, and I could tell they were all in whites like me. For me that was the first sure sign that we were in for something impressive and not just a time-and-place-bound joke.

Since Kev and I were the last ones expected, the ceremony began. Mike's familiar tom-tom started a quiet beat, then the sound of steps in the sandy ring, then the small light of tinder being blown on. In another minute a well-laid tent of dry wood was burning brightly, and I could see that the fire lighter was Rafe.

So far he was wearing the only Indian gear I'd seen tonight. It wasn't his eagle-dance wings though, just the new moccasins and a different breechclout made out of what seemed like real deerskin. The other boys had made theirs out of tan corduroy. At first he looked like a dressed-up boy, but then the firelight went to work. And soon it had given Rafe the air of genuine power he'd worn the first time I saw him here.

The tom-tom shifted to a faster beat, still muffled as if to keep our secret. And Rafe began a dance I'd never seen.

Whether it was a traditional piece like the eagle dance, I never knew. Nobody gave it a name or a background that night. And thereafter the way things went, I never thought to ask. If I'd had to guess, I'd have said it represented some version of the Prometheus story. Right off, it seemed to portray a fire stealer or at least a fire giver, somebody trying to help mankind with heat and light.

Or it could have been a whole-cloth invention by Rafe. All the gestures described some relation among the dancer, the starry sky beyond us, the blazing wood in our midst and the cold horizontal world at our feet. Then we four at ringside were woven into his final moves. He took a glowing stick from the fire and passed it slowly before us, eye level. I noticed that everybody's eyes went to Rafe; nobody watched the ember. As if we all half-expected him to strike and blind our eyes.

His face to be sure gave no hope of mercy. He looked as neutral as any great raptor, fixing its prey. But of course he returned the stick, harmless, to the fire. Whatever Rafe meant or whoever dreamed up the story he was telling, whatever he'd stolen and brought to Earth from whom and wherever, I at least felt glad. It felt like a serious blessing. One that would work, not just a pleasant hope.

Maybe the hint of theft that I felt in the dance was something born in Rafe, that built-in outlaw edge that clung to his every act. His eyes were so intimately connected to every other moving cell in his body that they were constantly changing the message they delivered. More than half the news he brought, that night, seemed to be various shades of joy—a deep delight. But there were odd moments when his eyes went cold again or his lips clamped in anger. What happened later makes it urgent to state that now as a fact.

Rafe Noren on that Thursday night was a changed boy again. This time he was really more joyful than not, though of course he never smiled.

I'd only seen him dance once before, not counting the time I caught him rehearsing. I've already described that uncanny change. But it's even more important to affirm that, though I'd recently felt his anger, I still thought his skills were finer on a second look. I knew then, as I know today, that this boy could be put on any stage anywhere and more than hold his own. No other male dancer of my experience, except the great Uday Shankar from India, lorded the common air with a nobler strength.

He ended again in a crouch. This time he knelt at Bright Day's feet. Day's hands reached out and pressed the boy's shoulders. Then the boy rose and left the ring quickly.

Day stood in the firelight and talked for no more than two minutes. He was dressed in full Sioux regalia—a deerskin shirt and trousers, intricately beaded, and a real eagle-feather bonnet that swayed to a life of its own with every step, in drafts from the fire and the cool occasional wind from the lake. In American dress Day had looked mildly pudgy. Now that was all changed. He was lean and growing taller as he spoke.

In later years I've been professionally hypnotized many times, mainly for memory exploration in connection with a series of etchings, scenes from my childhood. So I know I speak accurately in saying that by then, there in the ring, I was hypnotized and have no detailed memory of the words. I only know that Day didn't speak in Hiawathan sentimentalities about Brother Wind and Mother Stream.

He spoke of the fact that the tribe at Juniper, founded more than twenty-five years ago by Albert Jenkins and Mi-

chael Dorfman, still had fewer than twenty living members.
I think he said that all were inducted for "quiet valor" and
that six of them had died in war.

I'm sure of the "quiet valor." I thought how well it applied to Day but also Chief with his half-mad hopes and
Rafe with his whole battered graceful life. I wondered of
course where they saw it in me. Before my long nights with
Father, I'd have turned back the words. But that night at
Juniper, even with the ghosts of six dead men as my pre-
decessors, I stood still at least to see if the words would
settle on my head.

Day motioned to Chief and Sam. Mike had slowed the
beat again but kept it going. They rose and stood by Day.
Then Rafe materialized again out of the night and joined
them as an unquestioned equal. He was still wearing just
his breechclout and now a single down-hanging feather, and
I wondered how he could stand the chill. But it shocked and
then pleased me more to think that he'd kept this secret five
weeks—how these grown men had honored his courage.

One by one Day called up Kevin, Roger, Jim Todd and
me. Holding each feather in both his broad hands, as if it
were an actual burden, Day handed us all an eagle feather
bound at the quill end in buckskin. And he gave us each
our name.

Mine was Wachinton, which he said meant "Wise." I
tell that only for the cruel irony, triggered by me, that was
already blundering down upon us. I've said that Mike sometimes called me Wise One because of my lifelong interest
in the people we slaughtered to seize this land. So there's
no reason to think that Day or any of the older members
had a sarcastic intent. I do remember thinking that it
sounded surprisingly like Honest George. I can't remember

the other names, but Kevin's translated as something like
Lightning Hands and Roger's as Otter.

Then the drum returned. Rafe stepped from the front
bench back towards the fire. And in that simple three yards'
distance, he changed from boy to priest again. He danced
three wide turns around us, raking a quail-wing fan down
our chests. I tried to find the boy I knew. I was hunting the
boy that was scared in Asheville and that laughed here by
day or was forced to watch an ultimate horror on his own
home floor. But all I could see was this shadowy dancer,
held by whatever dream moved him on.

When we'd sat down again, Day stayed by the fire. In its
dryness it had already sunk to glowing coals. Day pointed
to Mike. The beat grew louder and Day alone sang the
prayer to Wakonda the Great Spirit which Mike had taught
us ten weeks before. The sound of the words in an Indian
mouth was different from what I'd grown to expect. And
that's what I still hear clearest from the night. A lone and
entirely dignified praise, no trace of begging.

All my life I've been an easy weeper. My eyes tear freely
at the least intensification of gladness, almost never at anger
or grief. I fog up for instance at TV commercials that ad-
vertise long-distance phone calls—sons calling their mothers who drown in tears. But I'm desert dry, though
sympathetic, at the sight of pain in the same room with me.
It's a genetic legacy from my father, whose sisters always
called him Works—short for Waterworks. So when Chief
and Sam came over to shake our hands, my face was a little
streaked. Then Day himself came and also ignored my embarrassment.

But when suddenly Rafe was there, with an army jacket
added to his breechclout, I thumbed at the tears.

So that of course was what he saw. He said "Wachinton, Wise Old Weeper." He raked my face again with the quail fan. Then he moved away with the older men, who vanished in darkness.

In another place and time, I might have felt excluded or wondered anyhow what plans they had that omitted me. I don't recall any envy however. Maybe it was a natural result of my ten weeks as father to fourteen boys, but the main thing I thought was "Rafe'll catch flu if he doesn't get dressed." Then in silence Kevin and I climbed back to our cabins together.

Kev spoke only when I turned off. "I'd never have guessed they could make it work."

I could only agree and, though the air was more than chilly by then, we sat on the steps of Cabin 16 and talked for a while. Since our Sunday together at the Thomas Wolfe house, we'd silently agreed to spend less time with one another. And while Kev had his Yankee coolness, I quickly felt that he now regretted the fact as much as I. Maybe he'd shied from my hot involvement in painting and Indian lore. I knew he shied from the sight I showed him that Sunday in Asheville, a goon half ready to rescue a knocked-up hillbilly girl and ruin his own fate. And I'd held back from a person who watched but really wouldn't judge me.

We both understood it was too late now. It's one of the first great adult sadnesses, coming to see what you've chosen to waste, an hour too late. Kev and I wouldn't know each other, a week from now. Something told me Kevin was thinking the same. And wild as I then was, I said "I'm sorry."

Kev waited and then said "Don't be."

It was the first heavy advice he'd given since steering me away from the Wolfe house, and somehow it made me laugh.

For all his distance Kev was a ready laugher, but this time he held back. He waited and then said "I know it just happened. I don't blame you."

I saw he'd misunderstood me but how? I didn't want to know.

Then he explained. "You probably saved Ray from a lot worse sickness. You heard him calling and I didn't. I asked Sam that night if I couldn't hitch into Asheville and stay, send you on back to camp. But Sam said 'Leave it.' And Ray came back, saying you did fine."

It had never dawned on me that, cool as Kev was, he might have felt trumped. But I only said "That was just how it broke." And then I said "Rafe's a unique creature." Since Asheville, I'd assumed that Kev didn't know the history of Rafe's disaster.

He said "I'd trust Ray Noren with my life."

If Kevin had chosen that moment to tell me at last that he was an incognito Trappist monk, he couldn't have surprised me more. So it was in shock that I said "It's his own life that's chancy."

Kev waited again and said "He won't make it."

At that point the chill of the night had reached me, and I gave a hard shake.

"Me too," Kev said and stood to go.

AFTER WHAT SEEMED AN ENDLESS BLACK HOUR IN MY BUNK with all the unconscious boys around me, I got back up, dressed warmly and went out to exhaust myself. Nothing specific was on my mind, though I did keep thinking *You'll leave here soon. You rescued the boy. And none of this time here will follow you home.* I walked all the way out to the highway. I toured camp twice and was still soaring high. By then I'd decided I was still responding to the ceremony, the way it had skated its thin-ice path to a safe completion. So I went back down to the ring and sat. I wasn't thinking about Rafe at all, certainly not about Rafe as a problem. By then I was thinking solely of me. I still had enough of the monstrous self-absorption of the secure child to be easily drownable in my own concerns.

In no special order, those concerns were the feasibility of life as a painter, the financial chances of study abroad, my duties to Mother, the hole in my heart that needed love and still had nothing but smiling compliant unhaveable Viemme. And always still, the deep-cut memory of my father's last breath, his dreadful fight to stay. It had not been a fight walked through by an actor enlarged on a screen but a man my size that I'd known since birth. The one man involved in my creation, ended for good and in my presence.

AFTER MAYBE A LONG HALF HOUR OF THAT, I HEARD A quiet voice say "Prayer is answered." It was unquestionably Rafe, though at first I couldn't find him.

He hove up out of the far lakeside, in dungarees and his army jacket. At first he stopped in the midst of the ring and stirred the ashes of our recent fire. Once he satisfied himself the coals were dead, he came and sat two rows behind me. Through what came next then, we both faced out towards the hidden audible lake. Our eyes never met—no reason to, in such thick dark.

Rafe said "You were right, a damned raw baby."

"Who?"

He said "Me." Then he waited. "Trying to punish you."

I said I noticed he had seemed cool.

Rafe said "Those two nights alone in Asheville turned out to be a lot more than I needed. I tried to blame you."

I said "You know I offered to stay. The world's mean enough; charity begins at home."

Rafe said "Faith and hope?" It sounded like a question. So I asked what he meant.

"Faith, hope, charity—the big three," he said. His random knowledge was always ambushing my expectations, and this was the first time I'd heard him move towards theology. Before I could think of a question to ask, he quoted St. Paul. " 'Though I speak with the tongues of men and of angels, and have not charity—' "

I couldn't get upstaged here. " '—I am become as tinkling brass or a sounding cymbal.' "

"What's a symbol?" he asked. "Like 'Home of the brave'?"

I didn't think to wonder if he was still teasing. I set him straight and also told him that St. Paul's *charity* meant *brotherly love*. Then I suspected he knew it all.

Finally he said "You sold that picture yet?"

"I've had several offers but no, I plan to keep it. Just after tonight, there's a lot here I want to remember."

Rafe waited. "I won't ask you then."

"What?—ask on."

He said "You gave it to me. I acted the fool."

By now I really wanted the picture, but I also knew my duty. Eventually I said, "You want it now?"

Rafe said "Please sir."

It pained me now that I'd fixed my mind on keeping the thing. But whatever the cost I said it was his then.

He waited again and then asked "Why? I'm a stuck-up kid. You're a great damned genius."

I reined him in hard. Without eating dirt on the spot, I said I was grateful for his respect but that I had just started on a more or less endless road, so I couldn't let him think I'd got there yet. Looking at his picture almost daily these three decades, I think I can now see what his lavish praise meant. First, the big portion of the world that lacks any talent for realistic drawing is pretty much in love with the few magicians who possess it. And second, my landscape is a plainly serious search for a large picture with a sizable mind or soul. It's at least no tyro's muddy colorslide peeled off the face of a photogenic view.

It was about then that Rafe said "You haven't climbed up to the prayer circle yet, have you?"

All along he'd gradually revealed a seasoned knowledge of all the camp's byways, and two hours ago I'd seen him at ease in the core of the place. But since Chief had warned us that the circle was for adults only, I'd strictly avoided discussing it with any of the boys. I'd thought of climbing up there by way of preparation for the induction. But then I got immersed in the picture and decided it was sufficient spiritual calisthenics for almost anything. I'd go when the campers were gone and I stood a chance of an unhurried hour. For now though, to answer Rafe, I took his own tack and said "That's classified."

He said "Please don't tell me you're one of those atheists."

I laughed at the thought of a swarm of atheists flying at Rafe. That would truly call for a mighty offensive by the

Youth Patrol. But I said "No, calm yourself. It's not something I'm any good at talking about though."

Rafe said "You don't think for a minute that your painting talent is some kind of accident made by a big anonymous chemistry set, do you?"

We seemed headed for a high-level discussion on the subject. I was after all a university student in the Bible Belt and had heard several thousand such debates. So I thought I'd head this one off by a simple statement followed by silence. "I was baptized in the Presbyterian church and raised there. When I was your age, the notion of God really gave me a fit. I felt he was watching me, round-the-clock. And his eyes were round and flat as a fish eye. They never once blinked. I didn't talk it over with anybody sensible. I didn't know anybody who was certified sane on the subject of God. So I settled on memorizing the Sermon on the Mount and trying to follow up on every last rule. Now I can wonder if Jesus meant it seriously—it's so damned hard, it's almost funny. But at your age I tried it. And Rafe, it nearly killed me—me and everybody standing near. So now I've pulled back, a lot, in the certainty department. You can rest assured though, I don't feel like a chemistry set, no, that somebody spilled together on the floor."

Rafe said "Have you thanked God for your picture?"

"Not in so many words. Whoever God is, I suspect he knows I don't think I invented myself or was built entirely by my parents' gonads. Surely he or it knows I'm deeply glad to have real work, any day I get it."

Rafe said "Amen." And nothing in the sound seemed to call for a smile, much less a laugh. Then he said "I've climbed up there the past two summers and said my piece and planted my stick."

"The place is for the staff, Rafe. Do Sam and Chief know?"

Rafe said "Not from me, they don't. But it's no damned Pentagon H-bomb secret. I'm all but grown. Hell, Chief himself took me up there the first time."

It didn't sound likely. "When and why was that?"

"Oh the second summer after my mother died. Pa had arranged for me to stay on, a few days after camp ended. And one of those afternoons, Chief found me swimming in the lake by myself. Looking back I can see that lone-wolf swimming was a lot more illegal than the prayer circle. Anyhow Chief didn't blame me. He called me to the pier and said 'Ray, go put on your overalls and shoes and meet me at the lodge in twenty minutes.' I've always obeyed him and he was there waiting. So I followed his stiff old legs up the mountain, and we wound up at the prayer circle. It was a tough climb for an eleven-year-old. But I'd heard about it already and was hell-bent to be there."

"I'm sure it's beautiful."

Rafe said "What isn't?—up here, I mean. Sure, it's got a nice view. But the sticks are the main thing, this whole big gang of sticks that grown men have prayed over. It was the best thing that had happened to me in more than a year. Hell, countless ages. I thought it proved people had a say in things."

There was a lot of silent time. Rafe seemed to be done with the subject. I thought that nothing could have sounded safer, on that kind of theme. So I calmly told him I was carving my stick and would climb up there once the campers were gone. That much of a confidence unfortunately warmed me to the theme. I went on and told him in fulsome terms about my wish to thank the powers for my own survival in Father's crisis, for my picture and the general safety of the summer and of course for his rescue. I didn't mention what was carved on my stick.

Rafe had listened patiently. Then he said "So you think there's a reason to pray?"

"You mean do I think God changes things if we ask him to?"

"More or less."

I said "Jesus says God always answers like the father he is. Recently though I've got a lot of my requests back with a big *no* stamped on them."

Rafe said "That's an answer."

"You bet."

He waited a good while and then, to my surprise, he laughed. "*No*'s about all I ever get."

I allowed as how that didn't seem the case—take his recent rescue.

He said "I never thanked you for that."

"You just did. Anyhow forget it, Rafe."

He took a while to say "What if I climb with you?"

For all our sharing, it sounded wrong immediately. First there was Chief's warning. Then there were my own increasing expectations for the visit. They were stronger than I'd admitted, even to Rafe. After the events of the past year, I'd begun to want a purification. I didn't feel bloody or filthy with sin, but I'd thought more and more of the kind of cleansing rites described in the Old Testament and all through Indian lore. A low small hut with a red-hot fire under rocks, a big iron kettle and a world of steam.

I needed something like a spiritual sweat bath. I wanted some way to shut down the past and to aim myself all over again for adult life. Hadn't I been in nursery school for fifteen years? Now I was primed for something like an ending to all that time and the setting out on a new vision quest. On this cold night though, I felt a fresh sadness for leaving a child whom too many others had left. And I had a new memory, of the equal place Rafe held in my induction. So I said "I'll ask Sam or Chief if it's all right."

Behind me Rafe gave a deep sigh which I heard as disgust. I'd walked out on him one more time.

It hit me hard. I've said that I was still in the fairly hot grip of an inevitable sense of failure for those last days of my father's life. It's a serious thing, agreeing to watch a loved one through so much pain and humiliation that you're helpless to ease, much less stop. You can't refuse it but it breaks something in you that will never heal. Plus I was trapped in the strong toils of a politely raised child's inability to refuse a request. In later years I've watched its power in the lives of my students. Even the most aggressive on-the-barricades hippie had trouble saying no if you asked him calmly and showed you cared. At that point I heard Rafe stand.

And it came to me suddenly that I wanted to know one more thing. I asked him to tell me his Indian name.

He said "I wouldn't tell you but you'd just ask Day. Day chose it, not me—Kinyan, 'Airborne.' "

So I faced him and, on faith, spoke towards a person I couldn't see. "You can guide me up."

He waited so long I thought he'd left. Then he said "How about Saturday, a while before sunset?"

Before I could answer I heard him leave.

But all the way back to Cabin 16, I felt much better. A burden was lifting. A chance was coming at final payment of all my ghosts, alive and dead.

* * *

THAT WAS THURSDAY NIGHT. I TAUGHT MY LAST CLASS FRI-
day morning and also put the last strokes on my picture,
signing it in the lower right hand corner with an almost
undetectable personal seal that I'd made from the letter *B*.
For the first and last time in my career, I added the date
VIII 54 and *Juniper*. I generally work for an image that's
not really locked to the calendar, no "Christmas Snow" or
"Easter Dogwood." But with this single picture, I needed
to own up to the things that made it—a time and place.

I was all but alone on the terrace when I finished. And
for the first of hundreds of similar times, I felt the almost
panicky initial loneliness of a maker. You've made the thing
with your own body, as much as any human baby. You did
it asexually but with a lot of passion and often with the
further strength you get from the freely offered sex of your
loved ones. You'll never get it back inside you, and still you
long for someone to share the tall wave of happiness.

There was nobody near, as I said, so I called to a camper
named Kip Espy, who was standing twenty yards away. He
loped over and I showed it to him.

He said "Hallelujah!" which was a good deal better than
nothing.

AFTER LUNCH I WENT TO INDIAN LORE. RAFE WAS OFF IN
his usual corner, refurbishing his head roach, a high flaring
crest that he'd made out of stiff hemp fibers. He acted normally, barely acknowledging anybody else's presence.

I mouthed the news that I'd finished the picture.

He nodded "Good" but gave no sign of rushing across
the hall to see it.

So I turned to binding the last few feathers onto my bonnet and listened once more to Day's council plans. More than anybody else I'd met till then, Day proved what big respect you command when you absolutely believe in your own acts. He couldn't pick up a chewing gum wrapper off the archery ground without making the act a part of his life, the one thing he was doing that instant and for a thought-out purpose. The only other examples I've seen of such focused care were in old Zen priests in Kyoto. All the more reason then to plan this council like the smashing of the atom. Day was also determined for us to understand its weight. This was no joke, not even a school play.

My boys had already gathered the wood for our campfire and built it on the periphery of the circle laid out on the playing field. In breechclout and bonnet I would rise and invoke the Spirit with raised arms; then I'd light our fire. Other counselors would follow suit till a wide ring of fires was ready for Rafe's new dance. At the peak of that, whatever it was, Rafe would light the central council pile. It was far and away the biggest pile of wood, and the Tsali boys had built it as their last challenge. Mike would play Indian melodies on his flute. Other groups would do short dances, Chief would speak briefly, Mike again would lead us in the Wakonda prayer. Then as the roar of the great fire subsided, Day would lead his Ghost Dance. And as a last-night special, the Chiefs would then welcome everybody—including any parents who'd arrived early—to the lodge for refreshments.

By the time Day finished with the plan, I was also done with the bonnet. But when I stood to leave, I was surprised to find that Rafe had left earlier. Again I was disappointed at not being able to show him the picture. It was nothing major, just the sense I described of being all dressed up

with no place to go or of having a substantial gift in hand
but with no receivers.

I went back to the art room for a check of my first elation,
and yes it was there. I'd finally painted a picture I respected.
Not good enough to be sure and, God knew, no universal
demonstration of the ''meaning of the Smokies.'' But it was
an honest effort, and it seemed unlikely to shame me. I had
a hot minute of wanting it back, of wishing that Rafe hadn't
forced my hand the night before by asking for it. But I feel
that way—what painter doesn't?—with every honest picture
I finish.

I took up a brush, dipped it in raw umber and wrote
Kinyan on the back, on the reverse side of my initials and
the date. For me, that cast the die. Now I could abandon
it.

THE REST OF THE DAY PASSED LIKE A GOOD DREAM, RIGHT
down to the end of the council. Completely on their own,
my boys stood up at the supper table. They all faced me,
George Harrell raised his hands to conduct, and all sang
''For He's a Jolly Good Fellow'' with the whole camp
watching. I managed not to boohoo, even when they
crowded around my chair, taking liberal pokes and crying
''S.B.D.!'' That tipped off echoes from most other cabins,
songs and pokes. But my boys were the spontaneous first,
and it's one of the few mitigating memories I have from
those final hours.

I DIDN'T SEE RAFE AT KEVIN'S SUPPER TABLE. AND WHER-
ever he dressed for the council, it wasn't in the Indian lore
room with the rest of us. We dressed ourselves but Bright
Day did all the makeup, to prevent silly mess by the younger

boys. Even there beforehand Day's immense gravity transformed the normal hijinks of backstage nerves into hushed expectancy. When we were finally ready, he gave us a last check. He asked us to be silent for half a minute and then led us out.

There was a far bigger crowd than expected, with maybe a hundred parents. And as the scenario unrolled, for some reason I worried more and more that Rafe would renege on his entrance.

But no, when the last of the circular fires was lit, Mike started the drumbeat and here came Rafe. Just in the twenty-two hours since the induction, he had thought through the story of his fire-bringer dance and had added new meanings. I no longer saw him as the human thief of divine fire but as a benign spirit, human enough to be mindful of the dark world's need for light and warmth but uncanny enough to be able to help us.

I no longer recall whether the American Indians had room for anything like angels in their theology. Most peoples do. But I know that as I watched Raphael dance, for the third and last time at the council fire, I hoped his dead mother had also known that the name she gave her only son was an angel's name before it was a painter's. A direct messenger from central control, for life or death.

Thinking back too, I believe Rafe made those final changes in the story he danced by the simplest of means, as in all born actors. I realize now that, just as he never asked me to turn my picture to words, I never asked him a single question about the story and meaning of his dances. But the shifting, almost reckless face he'd worn last night had eased now into a steady near-smile. It never beamed, never even hinted at frank delight. But I still believe it meant the world good, as the young man dancing surely did, for all his hard luck. And for whatever reason, his chest was painted but not his face.

Right at the end, whatever he'd tried to tell us by dancing, he moved to the high dark pile of wood, went down on a knee and—some secret way, without using matches that I could see—he started a flame. The small bright tongue licked upward quickly as Rafe stepped back. And in maybe under a minute, with him still standing a lot too close, the five-foot pile was one hot blaze. I didn't see him leave but, once the fire was bright enough, I noticed he was gone.

I'd watched some rehearsals for the culminating Ghost Dance, but they hadn't prepared me for what came next. When Bright Day rose he'd taken off his war bonnet and wore only a single down-hanging feather and a shapeless white ghost shirt that hung to his knees and concealed his beaded opulence. He went to the fire and chanted awhile in what I assumed was Sioux. And when the chant peaked to an obvious climax, he signed with a wide upward gesture for the dancers to rise.

Maybe twenty-five boys appeared from nowhere, with no trace of makeup and all in ghost shirts. At first people laughed a little. They did look a little too much like old-timey boys in nightshirts. But then the drum started and the dance began. It was hardly a dance, more like a rhythmic toe-heel walk around the fire, with signs to the sky. Day had said nothing to the parents and guests about the history of the dance or the desperate hope of Wovoka and the original dancers.

What would they have thought if they'd known of its hope for the withdrawal of the white man and the sending down of a red messiah? A poll of them all, mostly well-meaning middle-class Southerners, might possibly have found ten or a dozen who had some sense of guilt towards the red man. But almost too plainly Day had imparted that guilt, and the desperation of the original dancers, to the boys. By the time they finally stopped in place, with their thin trembling arms and stark faces raised to the stars, I almost expected the sky to answer.

When the drum weakened then and ended, I saw for the first time that one of the humblest dancers was Rafe. He'd somehow hurried into a shirt and joined the prayer dance with a face no longer giving but as needful as Day's and the first Ghost Dancers'. Strangely I told myself Rafe was happy. At least I knew he was his best self again and could take my decision.

THE SHOWERS WEREN'T EXACTLY SOMBER, BUT EVEN THE youngest boys showed they were still a little hungover. Again Rafe washed and changed somewhere else. None of us other participants though came fully to life till we'd changed into whites and joined the guests for refreshments in the lodge. Two of my sets of parents were there, wanting to hear how the session had gone and unanimously wanting to know who was the marvelous dancing counselor. Nobody guessed Rafe was a camper.

One of the mothers revealed to my surprise that she had been a member of Martha Graham's company ten years before. And she said "Seriously, Martha would be *impressed*. That boy knows more about fire than Vulcan! There's got to be a way to keep him dancing right on to the top. God never meant such a gift to be wasted."

It certainly sounded like what I'd read about Miss Graham's voice. I suggested she tell the boy in person and pointed to Rafe, standing alone near Mrs. Chief and the punch bowl. He hadn't smiled yet but he was relaxing.

She could hardly believe that an actual boy, in his wrinkled whites, had been the fire bringer.

THE SOCIAL HAD NEARLY ENDED WHEN CHIEF CAUGHT MY eye—I was also alone at the moment. He stepped over and congratulated me on "recent honors." Then he went straight to the point. "Bridge, I trust you recall the prayer circle?"

Short of telescopic surveillance I couldn't imagine how Chief knew who'd remembered and who hadn't. But you never questioned his sources; they tended to be infallible. I said "Yes sir, I plan to climb up towards sunset tomorrow."

I've mentioned my guess that Chief was more than a little deaf. There was often an unnerving wait between telling him something and seeing his face respond. Whatever the impediment, his unblinking eyes never wavered off yours. This was the longest such wait though, and it ended without his usual quick blip of a smile. He just said two unexpected things. First he nodded and said "You of all people," whatever that meant. And then he said "Alone, you understand. It only works alone."

Honest to God, at first I thought he meant that I shouldn't go up with Kevin. Chief had frequently spoken of his pleasure in our friendship. I had no reason to think he knew of my agreeing to go with Rafe, but the strange firm remark gave the final tap to my own decision. I assured Chief that I understood. And once he walked away, I looked for Rafe.

TO MY SURPRISE HE WAS STANDING ON THE PORCH OF THE lodge, in bright lamplight, in a group of his cabin mates.

Plainly at ease, here no more than half an hour after the council, he behaved as nearly like a normal boy as I'd ever seen. It was almost as weird a discovery as seeing him dance that first night or finding him bit by a snake, alone.

Before he saw me, a long deep laugh tore up from his belly. He cried out *"Never!"* Then he grabbed a short boy and knuckled his skull till the boy laughed too and begged for mercy. Then Rafe looked towards me.

I didn't speak but I beckoned to him.

At first I thought he might not have seen me. He gave a deep bow to the boy he'd knuckled, but then he pulled himself loose and came over.

Even as he walked, another boy said "*I* thought you were awful."

So I told him right off how much I admired the new dance. Then I said that his whole new generous-minded outlook made it easier for me to repeat what Chief had just told me—*It only works alone*. I'd have to go back to my original plan and climb to the circle tomorrow alone.

Rafe's wait was even longer than Chief's.

I almost thought he was going to turn and leave in silence, and I opened my mouth to start apologizing.

But finally he said "Suit yourself, O Wise One." He didn't look angry or sound sarcastic. He gave a quick wave and said "Abyssinia," which was that year's slang for "I'll be seeing you." Then he went back to his friends.

When they saw him coming, three of them fell hard to their knees on the concrete porch and salaamed his approach. Everybody else laughed, including Rafe.

IT SEEMS WORTH SAYING AGAIN THAT, EVEN TOWARDS THE end of the summer, I was not all that much concerned with

Rafe Noren. His eventual end was what made him grow so large in my mind. In fact, if I tried to estimate how much time I spent alone with Rafe, I'm sure it wouldn't come to much over an hour, except for the time together in Asheville. I've stressed my many other concerns, local and away. So that last night I could take Rafe's flip response at face value.

My boys had begun to collect around me for the walk uphill. They were still young enough to question the dark.

So I called to Rafe a final time, "Thanks again, Kinyan." He didn't look around.

And it struck me that our tribal names might be secret; no one had said. Then the thought of my seven shaggy boys hauled me off. Despite our rural setting they'd had most modern conveniences these past five weeks. About the only deprivation was haircuts, and they gloried in their shag. Once in the cabin—and once they'd looked under every bunk for skunks, coons or possums, not to mention snakes—we disregarded taps. I told them to get undressed as soon as possible. Then I doused our lantern. And we all lay back, really blind to each other, and talked our way through the five weeks together. Most of the memories to be sure were of mass jokes, individual humiliations or titanic farts.

But in a lull the youngest boy asked about the Ghost Dance—were any of those people really ghosts?

The other six decided that was hilarious and woke us all back up with laughter.

To bring us down fast, I began one of their favorite lights-out activities; I started a ghost story. This was one I hadn't told them yet, a favorite of my own childhood, from an uncle. It was called "The Old Woman All Skin and Bones." And from the first line, I had them captive—"There was an old woman all skin and bones, *woooo*.'' The moment I finished, the older boys would be unconscious, exhausted from the tension. And the younger ones, scared, would be eager for oblivion.

Once I detected a few slow breathers, I brought the story to a quick end and suggested a final round of Sentence Prayers. They were a popular devotional technique of the time, well before the Supreme Court made us reigning WASPs conscious of the anomaly of Christian prayer in an officially non-Christian country.

All my boys were apparently churchgoers. We'd tried this before so I knew what to expect. More than half of them would respond with unthinking thank-yous for sun, sky, birds and grass. A few more would turn up an unexpectedly nice detail, such as ''Thank you for us having dessert every night.''

The last boy—my oldest and favorite, George Harrell— said ''Thank you for Bridge being an artist and showing us where to look.'' He'd been in the art class and was one of the few who'd only in the last two weeks begun breaking out of a cramped view.

So lying there I knew for the first time the old teacher's frustration. Just as you cut a little path in their wilderness, you look up—they're gone and you haven't even told them the most important thing. Which assumes of course that you know it.

I'm glad to recall that when they got around to me for the windup prayer, I said ''Thank you for these young men and all their gifts.'' *Men* was stretching it, even with George.

But everybody said ''Amen'' and then Tim Tucker said ''What did I give you?''

''Trench mouth,'' I said.

And if I'd been all three of the Stooges, with buckets of whitewash, we couldn't have ended the night with more laughter. I let them giggle themselves to sleep, and they did so fairly rapidly.

That left me alone, above them in my upper. Lord, they'd trusted me. And wasn't that the absolute specific remedy to haul me back from the grotesque space I'd trudged through since winter? Calm genial trust, not howling need. I might not have made any money, but I'd got that much, and it felt a lot better than cold cash. Then and there again, I sent up thanks. I could never thank the boys; they'd look bored and run. I'd have to hoard it all for my work and pour it out there. Or for my own sons.

For another strange fact of my youth was the early conviction that I'd have two sons. A certainty that I'd participate in their making, I mean. I'd begun to suspect it in my early teens and would sometimes lie at night and think about their lives in detail, their names and hobbies. But I'd kept it to myself till, later that summer, for some quick reason I told my mother; and she hushed my mouth. She was from the old truly wise stock, who'd have never let you name them Wise One. They knew better than to foretell happiness or even mild success. Nothing riles the considerable amount of practical joker in God faster than that. Tell him you're happy, his ears go up and he thinks "You *were*." A thing I'd never have let myself think, even that young, was what good men my sons would prove to be.

BY TWO O'CLOCK THE NEXT AFTERNOON, ALL MY CAMPERS were gone. And there were only two boys left in camp. One was in the infirmary with an infected foot. He'd leave on Tuesday when his parents returned from France. The other

boy of course was Rafe. Kevin told me that Mr. Noren had
made arrangements for Rafe to stay with the Chiefs through
Sunday night. Then he'd fly his private plane into Asheville
and drive out to get him.

I would be gone by then. I'd arranged a ride east with
my fellow brave, Roger. But knowing that Rafe would be
around longer than I, I made no special effort to see him
during the busyness of arriving parents and departing boys.
Maybe I was hoping by then he'd forgot it, but really I
assumed he understood that the painting was his and that
he'd arrange to get it from me. The surface was still damp
but could travel, with care. I'd even stopped looking at it a
whole day ago. Brute cutoff is about the only way I can
agree to part from a favorite picture. I seldom even keep
photographs of them.

Kevin and I and two other counselors were planning to
drive into Asheville that evening for dinner and a movie.
Meanwhile I had four hours. Still wearing my whites I
stretched on the bunk for a nap, mainly a pause between
the weight of duty through ten weeks of minor boys and
this sudden heady freedom.

THE CHANCE OF SLEEPING THROUGH AN ENTIRE AFTER-
noon hour in Cabin 16 would have been inconceivable till
that moment—so much so that, when I bolted up awake at
three, I leapt to the floor in cold terror. What or whom had
I neglected? Rafe did fly through my mind—Kinyan and his
painting. But again I told myself there was no urgency. My
climb to the prayer circle was my only remaining plan. A
final Sunday service up in the Pasture would be the time of
farewells.

But the prayer circle now. Again like a child of my time,

I felt that a sacred rite called for good clothes. And there I stood in my whites. They were appropriate maybe but foolish for a climb. So I compromised by swapping the duck trousers for starched and pressed dungarees and the white buck shoes for climbing boots. Then I found the carved stick far back in my locker. And I took the long way, past the ring and over behind the lake, to avoid all meetings.

I SHOULDN'T HAVE WORRIED. CAMP WAS AS PEACEFUL AS an old battlefield. Even the crickets were under a spell. Apparently no one saw me. If so, they didn't speak. And I felt a small elation as I entered the evergreen thicket at the foot of the mountain. Even there I began to think I was foolish to wait till the last; surely I'd pass somebody coming down. Or somebody, maybe more than one, would be up there. Still the climb was easier than I'd expected. It was also silent, which boded well—no sounds of anybody else nearby, just the crickets slowing down as the air cooled slightly. There was only a little hand-over-hand scrabbling in the last hundred yards. So I was winded when I got there. But I was also glad in the knowledge that the summer had given me strength I never had before. In June I probably couldn't have made it.

MY FIRST THOUGHT ON GETTING THERE WAS *CHIEF WAS right*. It was worth it, worth a lot more than the climb seemed at first to cost me. There was no sign of anybody else, and the silence was even deeper up here. The circle itself was on the mountain side of an oddly flat natural shelf, maybe twenty feet broad. The far side was open, with no fence or railing. And that side gave the view, past a sheer drop, maybe two hundred feet straight down. I sat on the edge there and gazed out a long while. It was five minutes maybe before I realized that, even here on the edge of a fall, I was calm in mind and heart.

Serenity was the last skill I'd planned to acquire at a boys' camp. But here I was, alone again and glad to be. The view ran at a right angle to the one I'd painted, a long sweep right up the wild valley on the edge of which we'd perched so delicately all summer. If I'd climbed here earlier, I might have worried for the rest of the time at the prospect of an earthquake. The merest shrug by the ground would slough Juniper off its pretty moorings and send it and all its bodies tumbling five hundred feet deeper down. Not that earthquakes were likely. The Smokies are geologically among the oldest and most stable features of the American landscape. They're about as likely to shudder as a shark is to smile.

The broad tops of trees, especially the hemlocks, pretty well blocked a view of Juniper itself. There were scattered signs of former life immediately below. The Tsali boys had left too, but I could see a few of their sheds, and I wondered how many of those suffocated rattlers would ever wind up as belts or hatbands. Had they suffocated just to spend eternity in somebody's drawer? Otherwise it was me and a world I'd never made.

AND IN A QUARTER HOUR I FELT MORE PEACEFUL THAN AT any time since the long minute in which I watched my dead father before an intern barged in and found us. It was the kind of space and silence in which most people—and I in earlier times—would feel compelled to speak, calling out a name or some basic request to the singing air. Giving the Smokies a rave review.

That day though I was supremely ready to add my focused silence to the circle behind me. I walked back there and stood till I made out its actual perimeter on the ground. It was a good ten feet across. Where it touched the cliff side, there was a low hill of dirt with a few wild bushes. And it was there that the odd thicket of prayer sticks stood. There were maybe a hundred, most of them simple sticks—uncarved and unadorned.

When a man had troubled to plant his stick deep, it was still upright. Still dumbly reciting the prayers of young men long since grown, maybe some of them dead in Europe or Asia. A few sticks had been beat down by rain. It didn't seem advisable to prop them up. That would alter fate. A slow look also told me that there was not a single human name or other sign of pride, no defacements, no *Kilroys*. Chief had stated no rule to that effect and I was surprised. I was also glad that my own instinct had produced a snake and a rescued boy but no pointer to Bridge Boatner and his aims.

So I drove mine well down into the ground and packed the earth in hard around it. Then I went to the center of the circle and sat, facing all the sticks. With open eyes I thought my way back through these weeks. And at that moment there, the weeks and their contents seemed to become what I hadn't let myself realize till now, an unbroken blessing. The one word *healing* kept coming to mind. I remember, after maybe ten minutes, saying to myself a thing that seemed directly inspired, not just a wish—*This power will follow you for long years to come*. I wasn't about to look the power straight in the eye and give it a name. But I knew I'd felt it always. And as I said, I knew then and there it wouldn't leave me. So far, I was right.

The first night of the summer, I'd promised myself to come up here and dedicate my mind and body to finishing my father's cutoff life. Two and a half months later, I was here but not for that purpose. Father was himself and sadly he was gone. I was his unfinished son, alive and working. So here at the end, I made a vow to spend my whole life, if fate agreed, in using the one real block of capital I knew I'd been given. And that of course was my old need to watch those parts of the world that caught me, then to copy them out for others less patient or with eyes less lucky.

WHAT HAPPENED THAT NIGHT, HARD AS IT WAS, AT NO TIME entirely canceled my vow. In the short run the strangest fact for me was the fact of survival. At a time when the sum total of my actions—my hollow eneouragement of Rafe, the slow parade of feebly thought-out spiritual hints that I trailed past him—might have called for me to quit the Earth too, I balked. I loved myself too much. I stayed and lasted. Above all else I worked. Men more gifted than I have resigned from life for lesser mistakes, van Gogh for one and a sad lot of poets.

But in under a week from my hour in the circle, I was working again in my mother's house. And I worked not only because of my errors but with them, as instruments. It may be only a simple fact to claim, here now more than thirty years later, that Rafe Noren's life is present deep under the lines I've drawn and especially the shadows. And more, I can sanely claim that every good and usable thing I learned in that valley and on its heights is in me now, compacted, altered and shaped by time.

* * *

KEVIN AND I AND OUR TWO FRIENDS DROVE BACK INTO CAMP at one in the morning. We'd been to Asheville, eaten real steaks and seen "Seven Brides for Seven Brothers," an appropriately joyous rural stomp. Then we'd eaten an early pancake breakfast. Chief's hold on us was still strong enough to rule out beer. The rest of our lives would be time for that. So we turned off the highway and in through the camp gate, tired but happy with overstuffed bellies and empty minds. As we crested the last rise and saw the lodge, there were two men standing in the road, with their backs turned. We were surprised and needed a moment to see it was Chief and Sam. My own only thought was "Thank God we're sober."

They came straight towards us.

Roger stopped and leaned out the driver's window and said pleasantly "Nighthawks, I see."

I knew he meant the two men; Chief prided himself on bed by nine. But something in Chief's new fluid movements made me foresee trouble. Since late afternoon something had smoothed Chief out. He was suddenly almost a graceful mover. In another few seconds I saw it was his speed. Something had struck him. He was moving at half speed.

He set both hands on Roger's window ledge, bent to see us all and said "We've had a tragedy, boys."

He'd never called us *boys* before. I knew at once that the word itself was some kind of gauge of the pressure he felt. But even my anxious mind thought only "Mrs. Chief or Mike," somebody old.

After that Chief lost his voice for a while. I've mentioned a new slowness. His skin had also aged ten years since afternoon. His head withdrew and he took a step back.

Roger said "May we help you, sir?"

Sam leaned in then and said "Young Ray Noren's had a very grave stroke."

Stroke? Strokes killed old men, like Franklin Roosevelt nine years ago or my own grandfather. Or it ruined their speech or halved their bodies. At that we all got out to hear the news. I only remember telling myself there was some mistake. It was somebody else. Rafe had earned more mercy from the world.

Sam looked to Chief. "You want me to tell it, sir?"

Chief shut his eyes and nodded.

So Sam began. Simm Burwell, the riding counselor, had climbed to the prayer circle right after supper. It was just before seven and still daylight. When Simm got there he went like everybody else to the valley side and watched the view. Nothing felt unusual, no strange sounds. But when he went over to plant his stick, he saw a body lying behind the thicket. The face was up and Simm knew him at once— "Simm said he'd have known Ray anywhere, looked just exactly like he did last night when he lit the big fire." He was wearing his whites, and they weren't even dirty. No sign that he'd struggled on the ground. In his hand was a stick he hadn't used yet. Simm said his skin was hot to the touch. Not feverish but hot as a working man. No sign of blood or even a wound.

With good sense Simm rushed back to camp. It would take more than one man to carry Rafe down the few steep yards. But within half an hour, they had him at the bottom where the nurse checked his heart. It was beating weakly. So Simm, Chief, Sam and the nurse all took him to Asheville in the station wagon.

The doctor who saw Rafe through the snakebite was there. It didn't take long till he came to the lobby and told them plainly that Rafe had suffered a massive cerebral hemorrhage. He urged them to come back out here and wait. It might be minutes. It might be years. Chief wanted to stay, and they all waited in the lobby till midnight. Then the doctor came back and said the same thing. No change, go home.

Till then in Sam's story, I hadn't even thought of words. My mind was too cold. But now I asked "What's the real prognosis?"

Chief looked to Sam.

Sam said "Very bad. If we could just have found him sooner. The doctor said that, by the time he saw Ray, pressure from the internal bleeding had already done too much brain damage. There's really so little spare room in the skull. He said he felt there was no chance of Ray waking up. But he also said that, with this strong a body, the boy might well linger for years in a coma."

I said "We can pray he doesn't get that."

Chief spoke up at last. "No, we leave that to God."

WHICH WAS WHAT WE DID. WE COWED IN PLACE AND waited for an end. At Sam's suggestion we brought our sleeping bags down to the lodge and slept on the floor. Or got still and dark. I heard a few sighs from Roger, Kev, Simm and Possum but no real sleep. My mind still wouldn't work. In some act of kindness I'd learned that night, it went entirely flat and gray. Very few words came and no strong feelings. No blame or guilt or grief or hope, just a blurred refusal to believe the worst. Surely I wouldn't be struck this hard twice in one year. Even then, you'll notice, it was all about me.

I figured the others were deep asleep, but suddenly Kevin sat up and said *"Wrong."*

It woke everybody. Simm said "Wrong what?"

But Kev had forgot. It was part of a dream. Anyhow he lay back, then laughed and finally told everybody about the horse, him finding his three boys humping the mare. Back in the dark I cringed at his timing. But once he got to the laughing end, he said "It was Ray that saved their necks."

Simm said "Doesn't sound like their *necks* needed saving."

Then Kev told a story I hadn't known. He said "I was going to go tell Sam and get his advice. But the boys ran to Ray, and he waylaid me walking down here. He challenged me to a tetherball match. To cool my jets, I thought 'Why not?' But Ray beat me, hands down. I congratulated him and turned to leave, but Ray said 'Whoa there. You headed to Sam?' I said 'Sam or Chief.' Ray said 'It would stop Chief's heart right *now*.' I said 'Ray, this is no problem of yours.' He laughed and said 'Kev, you don't understand. You lost your chance.' I begged his pardon. He said 'We played that tetherball match to see if you got to be a damned spy or not. You lost and thereby lost your spy license. You are now Camp Juniper's luckiest man.' I asked him how so and reminded him, in any case, I hadn't agreed to play by his rules. Ray said 'Maybe not but see it this way—I'm helping you spare a poor kind lady's name. She was just doing her bit for teenaged morale.' I asked 'What lady?' He meant the mare."

Simm said "Adelaide? Lord, she's been serviced by so many boys, she backs up every time she hears one speak."

That led to a string of other stories about Rafe. I no longer felt they dishonored him, and I knew more stories

than all of them together, but I let them talk and just lay
still. I even think I dozed in and out of the long discussion.
I was wide awake though when Roger spoke.

He'd been silent like me, but he finally said "I feel like
he's gone."

I had to speak then. I said "No don't." Just saying the
words might force him to go.

Roger said he was sorry. It had just passed through his
brain that instant.

And at that point everybody gave up hope, including me.
Nobody said so and I at least denied it to myself. But we
knew that Roger had told the truth. And somehow that let
everybody sleep. Even I slept maybe three whole dark hours.

RIGHT BEFORE DAWN SAM OPENED THE DOOR. SOMEHOW
in sleep I knew he was coming. I knew what he'd say, and
I managed to say in my mind *Please, God*. It was the closest
I'd come to taking his name in anything more than vain for
some months. I remember noticing that Sam had shaved.

He opened his mouth and it stayed a black hole till he
finally said "The doctor just called. Ray died at four-thirty.
I've reached his father and he's flying in early. Mrs. Chief
says everybody come to the house as soon as you've washed.
She's cooking breakfast."

Even though we'd eaten one breakfast already, that was
some kind of blessing. The ancient balm of food on grief.
Remember how, at the end of the *Iliad*, old Priam and
Achilles—mortal enemies for years—settle the transfer of
Hector's corpse? Then they sit down to eat, exhausted but
hungry men again.

* * *

VERY LITTLE WAS SAID AND AT FIRST I WAS GLAD. THEN after coffee and a little hot food, a pocket of guilt burst inside me. At first it was mindless, no logic or reason. Next it made me feel like a bereaved family member who was getting no notice. I didn't say so. I joined the others in eating corn fritters with maple syrup, bacon, a world of fresh milk and strong coffee.

Shocked as we were, Chief forgot to say grace.

By the end of the meal, though, Mrs. Chief remembered. She said "Oh Albert, we didn't give thanks."

That seemed almost worse news to him than Rafe's. He rose in place and, thank God, didn't suggest that we touch, no chain of hands. I might not have made it. He said "Great Father, we're speechless here beneath this unfathomable stroke of your hand. Your will be done. And we thank you for all that's left to the living. Help us see what it is and where to find it."

I remember wishing I'd ever known a preacher with a mind that fast, that hugged the ground of life that close and responded that soon.

No one said "Amen" but Day, who just then stood in the door.

As Sam began to portion out duties for the general cleanup, Chief's eyes called me over. He said "Bridge, meet me in the *Thunderbird* office in ten minutes please."

I was still too stunned to be afraid. I could only guess what he'd ask me first.

AS I WAITED IN THE OFFICE I'D CLEANED SO THOROUGHLY two days ago, I came much closer to breaking down than I had before. Again not from guilt and any kind of anger but just from the weight of the year behind me. I was twenty-one years old, but *three score and ten*? Who on Earth could stand it? I remember thinking I'd burn the picture. I'd never be able to see it again, and a funeral pyre might just be called for.

When Chief came at last, his first question was "Had Ray said anything to you, last week in Asheville or back out here, about any such climb?"

I had no master plan for a cover story. I simply took one step at a time. "Sir, he asked to climb up there with me late yesterday afternoon. I told him no." Strictly speaking that was true.

Chief said "Good for you. I'm relieved. He asked me about it too, more than once in recent years."

I said "Sir, Rafe told me you showed him the way."

Chief's old stiffness returned; he lurched back. "When?"

"He said he climbed up there with you several years ago."

Chief actually smiled. He had caught his boy in one more tale. "I promised I'd take him when he was sixteen, if he came to Tsali or even as a visitor. But I plainly said 'Not one day sooner.' " Chief went to the mimeograph machine and examined it closely with a clean forefinger. I'd left it spotless. Suddenly he turned round, faced me head-on and said "Did you love him?"

A hand grenade lobbed through my teeth could not have hit me harder. Thirty years ago people didn't just wind up and pitch such curves. I quickly tried to read Chief's meaning, his Christian background, his pithy sermons. I said "I loved what I saw deep in him."

Chief's big eyes filled and he nodded fiercely. "Can you give it a name? What was it, Bridge?"

To this day now, I couldn't tell you where I got what

came. I said " 'Though I speak with the tongues of men
and of angels and have not charity—' "

Chief kept on nodding. "Yes, say it. *Say* it."

I quoted onwards as far as I could. Then Chief took over
and, between us, we made it somehow to the end. " 'And
now abideth faith, hope and love, these three. But the great-
est of these is love.' " We both substituted *love* for *charity*.

I said "What I mean is, love worked Rafe."

Chief nodded "To death. It absolutely killed him."

Again I wonder where we got such words. Never underestimate the combinations at the fingertips of any two men
raised on the King James Bible, a lifetime of sermons and
hundreds of hymns. I thought at the time *Maybe we are two
fools babbling this early, or maybe we're inspired or dead
with exhaustion or all the above*. I can't speak for Chief;
but maybe I meant that Rafe Noren lasted as long as he did
because he plainly prized the world, all he could see that
was not stingy, joyless or cruel. I still think the same. Anyhow not even adult men should get full blame for what they
say in the wake of such news. At least we didn't say Rafe
was better off.

THE MOMENT CHIEF LEFT I WANTED TO RUSH TO THE OF-
fice. Even in the presence of Clara and the secretary, I'd
call Viemme in Maine or Murmansk. I'd find her this time,
if it took all morning or into the night. It felt as urgent as
hauling Rafe to Asheville the day of the snakebite. I didn't
yet know how Death and Eros use the same wires in our
sparsely wired body. God also often employs the same circuit. So I actually locked the *Thunderbird* door and was on
my way. I would find a person whose body I knew, a woman
that trusted her body to me and would trust it again, more

fully now. And with the simple sound of her voice, I'd somehow cool the fever that burned me.

But there was Mike Dorfman at the office door. His eyes were red and, without a word, he pressed both his hands down hard on my shoulders.

I said "This just about ends it, Mike." I had no clear idea what I meant.

He nodded hard and said "Wachinton." Then he stepped back to look. Like Chief, Mike could stare down a charging rhino.

I managed to bear it without shying off.

So he said "Wachinton" again and moved away.

I waited in place till Mike was well gone. More than anyone here, I knew I'd miss him in years to come. I also knew we'd never meet again. I was right in both things. Then I turned and went on uphill.

WE COUNSELORS SPENT A DAY STORING THE BEDDING, sweeping out cabins and clearing the grounds like punished children. By now my mind kept saying I'd caused it. If I'd done my job and discouraged Rafe's climb. If I hadn't been so on-fire in his presence, I might not have pressed him to plan a climb. A child just back from a rattlesnake bite— who did I think I was dealing with? If after all I had understood that Raphael Noren was still a child and couldn't consume a full man's diet, he might be a man among us now. But who was a man? Hardly me, that day. I was in deep trouble and nowhere to turn.

LATE IN THE MORNING I SAW KEV MOVING DOWNHILL WITH something in his arms. I was powerfully tempted to call him back and tell him, to let him decide what I should do next. Go to Chief, confess and take the blame? But what here and now would blame amount to? It could only add up to deeper grief for a few helpless people. Then something stopped me from calling out. But I ran to catch Kev. And when I got there, I saw what he had—a cardboard box half full of Rafe's things.

Kev had packed the few clothes and belongings. And he opened the lid without my asking. "Anything of yours here?"

"Oh no," I said truly. And I knew not to rummage. Rafe had told me his dance regalia was stored in Mrs. Chief's room. He said he didn't trust them anywhere else—"these boys would just ruin that as well." But laid in the top of the box was the single feather he'd worn, pointed down, after dancing in the tribal induction and the Ghost Dance.

When I picked it up, Kevin said "You keep it."

"You think I should?"

"If you want it, you should. Nobody will know."

Kev was righter than he would ever guess, but I chose to obey him. I took the feather and the beaded headband back to my cabin. After all Rafe had willed the headband to me; the eagle feather came attached. And hadn't the child been named Kinyan, Airborne? To this day I have it, a strong wing feather wrapped with buckskin at the quill end and the cowhide headband, beaded in blue. Moths have chewed at the edge of the feather, but I mean to go on keeping it still. It hangs on a nail by the painting itself. They'd have lasted longer, stored behind glass; but I wanted them close and still don't regret it.

RIGHT UP TILL I LEFT JUNIPER, NO ONE ASKED ME IF I'D ever heard Rafe speak of headaches or weakness. The doctor had told Sam that the autopsy showed Rafe had suffered the rupture of an aneurysm. He also said that sudden deaths in childhood were often the result of congenital weaknesses in an artery wall—children who fall off a low sofa and die on the rug, football players in light spring practice. So maybe Rafe's problem had been there since birth; maybe it was weakened by snakebite or maybe by the climb to the prayer circle. Or maybe not, to any of those. The doctor apparently was one of the thousands, rarer then than now, who see malpractice suits in every bed and are more concerned with shielding their funds than in understanding a fact as plain as one boy's death and the rings it left in the water around him.

I KEPT MY OWN QUESTIONS TO MYSELF. I'D LEARNED, WITH my father, not to try to answer every big question the moment fate asks it. Maybe strangely, the thing that concerned me most in my last hours at camp was what to do with my painting. The urge to burn it had luckily cooled. I could give it to Chief, for the lodge fireplace. Or leave it for Rafe's father, Mr. Noren. But nothing I'd heard about him made me want to. In any case it would raise more questions than I needed to face.

Roger said we had plenty of room in the car.

And at the last minute I went to get it. As I was leaving the art room, I saw Day across the hall. He was sitting by a window, just looking out. So I went in to say one more goodbye.

Day called me Wachinton too and thanked me for my presence in his classes. He wondered if I'd be back next summer?

I had to tell him that was unlikely. I hoped to be in Europe.

He gave no visible response to that, and I was on the verge of turning to leave when Day said "Were you the one who told him to go?"

It was almost the longest sentence I'd heard him say, and again it struck me hard. My mind was just calm enough to assume that *go* meant to go on the climb, not the way towards death. And I also could hear that no blame was involved. I said "Why would you think that?"

Day's face was as blank as the sky outside. "He did what you did."

I expressed my genuine amazement. Rafe had seemed as different from me as anyone I'd known. Then I asked how Day knew that I'd climbed to the circle.

He said "One of your boys told me about the stick you carved, with the snake and the head of Kinyan."

So much again for my earlier sense of being ignored.

Then Day expanded. "I knew him from the summer his mother was killed. From then till last year, he was the same—bitter and hurt. He was different this summer, more serious and always laughing. I saw him watch you, every day in here. Everywhere he went, he watched you work. When you were gone, he could talk and move like you."

"Yes, he teased me a lot."

Day said "Not teasing. Last week when he picked your tribal name, he said he needed a brother like you. But you were too late."

I could barely hear it, it cut so deep. Rafe had picked my name? But I had to know more. "Did Rafe say I was too late or did you?"

Day said "Not I."

I wanted to get out fast forever but held my ground and told myself that this was food for thought for a far distant day. Rafe thought I'd have made a useful brother, but I came too late. The news was much too charged to handle, now at least. And since I'd still heard no trace of blame in Day's voice, I turned the tables. "Were you the first one to teach him dancing?"

Day nodded and actually smiled. "The first summer I came here was the summer I mentioned. Ray had seen his mother killed. The day he met me here in this room, he drew me aside and told me the story. He asked me to tell nobody else. He said he wanted an Indian to know." At that Day smiled again, for maybe the third time all summer. It looked as natural as if he did it daily. "I led him down to the ring that day and began to teach him. Someway I started at a very high level, with the eagle dance. I've never known why. I'd had classes for other boys. But they never learn it. It was a thing I knew I could give Ray. Ray had the long legs for it and the mind. And he did learn, fast. Better than anybody I've seen, except my older brother Chester Bad Boy. I'm not a good dancer, but I know the old ways and can teach the right boy. Ray was right. And I think it helped him at first, for a while—a few minutes at a time. It was what I could give him."

I said "Day, it was half the boy's life."

He moved away, back to the window. He said "Oh no. You're kind but wrong. Nothing helped Ray."

How was I going to leave it at that? Who, with white skin, could stand it? Yet I saw Day had finished. He believed himself. He'd built that fine tall dancer in vain. Now it amounted to nothing at all—for the Spirit, the dancer or the dancer's own people. I put my right hand out again.

Day took it briefly and said he hoped my paintings never stopped.

I'm glad to say I told him he'd taught me more than anybody else all summer. I meant it too, except of course for Rafe. And Day knew that, more than anyone else.

THE OTHER FAREWELLS WERE ALMOST SILENT, NO EMPTY promises to stay in touch. Some of us even waved across space, no pretense of more. And literally nobody said "I'll write" or "Come on to see me." If Rafe had lived, he and I anyhow might have swapped Christmas cards a year or so. As it was, we all slunk out like dogs. Good dogs to be sure but caught out of place, with our dignity down. Within two years I'd lost contact with everybody there, and now I don't know a single whereabout or even who's alive.

Kevin, I heard, joined the CIA and sank out of sight in that bottomless hole. About ten years later I happened to be at an airport near his mother's home and called her on impulse. She claimed to recognize my name and said that Kevin was "military attaché" at the embassy in Finland; they're invariably spies. Chief and Mrs. Chief, I know are dead. Alive, they'd now be pushing a hundred. Good Mike Dorfman is dead as well. Sam's in his eighties, retired in Asheville.

I've recently seen brochures and posters that say Bright Day still works for his people. I've made no effort to make contact; but apparently Day now tours the college circuit with a young male dancer, his adopted son. Day "lectures, recites and chants the Old Way." The son dances. On the latest poster he wears eagle wings. His name is Beau Fitzhugh, but he looks like an Indian.

I guess they're riding the modest wavelets of national guilt for the red man. Maybe I've said it too many times here; but once more, it's a guilt that is still unthinkably slight for the national sin that outshines slavery, if you're measuring sins—which is always our favorite pastime after sports. At nearly sixty Day must look grand as old Chief Joseph of the Nez Percé, surrendering at last after fleeing with all his women and children through ice and snow so that white Montana could now sleep safe, all thousand or so palefaces in cabins—

> *It is cold and we have no blankets. Our little children are freezing to death. I want time to look for my children and see how many of them I may find. Maybe I shall find them among the dead. Hear me, my chiefs, I am tired. My heart is sick and sad. From where the sun now stands, I will fight no more forever.*

Till I started this I'd fought no more, not that old fight of Rafe's last days. Now I've written it down because Rustum Boatner, my younger son, is majoring in art history at Colgate. Three weeks ago towards the end of spring vacation, he told me he was planning a senior thesis next year on my early work. It turned out his teacher knew a lot about my things, especially the early pictures; and he encouraged the project. Once I'd recovered enough to speak, I showed Rust the messenger sketchbook again. Both boys were attracted to it as children. Children have a lot of evidence, pro and con, as to angels.

We even looked at the old Smokies landscape over my bed, "The Meaning of Things." It had also been a favorite of Rust's since childhood, and he got it down to dust and measure. At which point he saw Rafe's name on the back— *Kinyan* in umber, which started me talking. That led Rust to questions. They went so deep that, to my surprise, they gouged raw meat. To be sure, I'd known that parents open their pasts to children at dire peril. And whenever I've dared it, I mostly wind up slamming the door in under three minutes.

But Rafe had never come up here before, so when Rust started I didn't plan to balk. Still after three rounds of painful questions—who was Kinyan, what had he meant and where was he now?—I had to call a hasty quits. My son's curiosity was so apparent though, and his courteous need for help was so genuine, that I agreed on the spot to a deal. I'd try to describe it all for him, as true as I could, in some bearable form. He and his brother Hugh could file it.

I SAY I HADN'T FOUGHT, NOT THE OLD INNER FIGHT ABOUT why Rafe died. What I mean is, the intervening years were no darkling struggle with inner blame. But my work, as I said, has been partly shaped by it. The drawings of imaginary messengers became a series of tempera paintings that were my introduction to success. Some of them hang in surprising places, surprising because I hadn't thought that sort of visionary thing could be communicated in Eisenhower's and Nixon's pastel fat-cat America. I've made almost yearly painting trips back to the North Carolina mountains—the Blue Ridge, the Smokies and sometimes on up into Virginia towards the Shenandoah. But I've never gone back to Juniper itself.

Two years ago a student of mine, who'd been a counselor well after my year, was driving nearby and decided to check. The Chiefs were long dead, and their whole life's work is slowly rotting in weeds and saplings. Some of the older cabins are already roofless. Cedars are growing in the archery ground, where the Ghost Dance was. The lake is choked with waterplants now, the result of nitrogen pollution in the streams. Only the campfire ring is unchanged. Some of the wooden benches are rotting, but the hemlocks above have thickened considerably, and their shade keeps the dancing floor bare and ready. Knowing nothing of my story or Rafe's, my student even clawed his way up to the prayer circle and reported that, to his surprise, dozens of prayer sticks were still upright. His among them.

Of course I didn't ask about mine. He wouldn't have looked that carefully. Anyhow the stick would be thirty-odd years old. Surely it's gone. As you now see, I've got memories of the place that are clearer than any confirming snapshot. As much surely as any man alive, I know what a burning glass Juniper could focus on susceptible minds—the beautiful place coaxed from a wilderness, Chief himself with the blue flame eyes and all they foresaw, Mike and Day on the ramparts of a noble dead cause, Sam and Kevin both sane as judges, the girl at Thomas Wolfe's house in Asheville, so much and so many more.

AND RAPHAEL PATRICK NOREN. I LEARNED HIS FULL NAME from the obituary in the next year's first *Thunderbird*. Chief sent it to me with the briefest note in his masterful hand, "I wrote this myself, hoping to make it worthy of the boy."

In conclusion the obituary said

> *No one can know Ray's final prayer. I rest in the certainty that it was not selfish. To an unbelievable extent for one his age, he was involved with life beyond himself. He had not understood it fully yet, but he loved his neighbor. And his rich endowment as an Indian*

dancer sprang partly from that, his knowledge of other rooms in creation. An eagle in flight, a dying stag, the lord of fire!—that all these things and a myriad more were in easy reach of the mind of a boy so young and untraveled! Surely his last breath was for another soul.

And surely Raphael Patrick Noren will last in the hearts of all who were lucky to cross his path and share it a ways. More than many old men I have known, Ray had seen most of life. A happy marriage and satisfying parenthood may have been the only omissions from a rich run of years. That knowledge alone may help us now in the diminished natural world he cherished.

A day seldom passes that one of us here—Michael Dorfman, my wife, my niece, myself—doesn't say "I thought I heard old Ray just now." No doubt we have heard him and will do so always.

To my surprise the word *old* rang true. Rafe was an old soul in all good senses and some of the sad. But when Chief said he'd hear Rafe's voice *always*, he slipped uncharacteristically. A man of his faith should have known to say "I hope to hear him, as long as I live" and Chief is dead. Bridge Boatner's alive awhile longer, to be sure. He works most days to copy things that count in the world. So far the things are mostly people, some noble animals, a few natural objects and occasional disguises of God. Whoever God is, he or she or it still intends to keep Rafe Noren alive on this Earth till Bridge Boatner stops. Only the pictures may last awhile longer.

So now I've told both my sons about him and asked that they keep my first earnest landscape in the family after me. They've promised they'll draw peaceful straws at my death and keep it in three-year relays thereafter. Even my

great-grandchildren et cetera may have Rafe's name in place
on their walls, though hid on the back of a young painter's
picture and disguised in the one strange word *Kinyan*.

Maybe these words will also last—not till the sun burns
out of fuel, begins to swell and then ends Earthly life. Even
back at Juniper I wouldn't have claimed that. But a few of
them might outlast me awhile. I mean also to give this to
friends. More than most people I've watched through the
years, I've had miraculous luck with friends, more friends
in fact than I can maintain. The days and nights aren't long
enough to keep up with them and thank them for kindness.
Many of them like Rafe are heavy with gifts to give the
world outside them. They're painters, sculptors, composers,
poets, dancers, actors, singers, priests, saints and one actual demon who managed to freeze every life he touched,
though he wrote grand music. I've had the further luck to
know many of them in their youth.

I said at the start, I hoped I learned the right thing from
Rafe's death. I think it was this. Inspiration is the Holy
Ghost's business, not mine or the Pope's or this month's
mistress. We humans can say things like ''Never use blue
in your shadows.'' Or ''Yellow, not black, is the color of
death. Think long and hard before using yellow.'' We can
offer bed and board to the gifted young or careful praise.
With extreme care and caution, we can even offer to please
their bodies.

But with young artists now—and most other people, if
the truth be told—I take a strict care that in my ignorance
I didn't take with Rafe. I don't go sounding off in their
hearing with odes to the Muses, the thrills of high art and
the endless joy of self-realization. I don't throw gasoline on
anyone's fire, however thirsty or feeble it looks. The keep-

ing, feeding and fanning of flames is nobody's business but the gifted youth's and his or her God's. Any help I give beyond patient witness is likely to be mischief, whatever the light.

NO YOUNG PERSON KNOWN TO ME, NOW OR PAST, HAS thrown a stronger light than Rafe Noren or farmed more corners of the world he touched with serious laughter. Young as he was, it was laughter launched with open eyes in full sight and knowledge of the final jaws. All he left was memory in a few dozen minds, some of them dead also. I make that dubious claim of course without really checking. If I could only find a handful of veterans of Rafe's years at Juniper, we could raise a memorial to him, there on the cliff in sight of that valley. For whom to see? A few passing hawks. No, human minds are what he touched. And surely I'm not the last soul alive who still remembers that strong a signal.

Even I though, with a painter's sight, can no longer see Rafe clearly, face-to-face. The odd thing is—and I just discovered it, writing this—I can see Rafe out of the corner of my eye, in peripheral vision. It's only when I try to stare straight ahead and catch him full-face that he steps aside and will not be caught. No doubt his father had a few snapshots. Is he still alive, with his latest wife? Where would they be now?

I once felt tempted to contact the man and ask for a picture to draw from, while I still had enough live memory to help me. But then I knew that the simplest contact would start me telling white lies again. So I kept my peace, not even a courteous sympathy note. Mr. Noren had never seen me. Who was I to wade out into his life when he had taken one more cold shaft through the midst of his heart? Or maybe he hadn't. Maybe it was more like a business loss, regrettable but soon behind him. To find that out would be worse still. And since I can no longer see Rafe's face in the necessary light, I can't even try to paint his portrait. He was too solid, too much a real boy, to risk guessing at as I guessed at another real brand of messenger.

I KEPT MY PEACE, AS I SAID, TILL NOW. WHOEVER ELSE IN fourteen years he managed to reach, Rafe Noren marked me. Not a wound or a scar but a deep live line, like the velvet burr in the darkest shadows of Rembrandt etchings, the ones I've mentioned where demons lurk. Let this be clear—never have I let myself for one instant think that Rafe died so that I might work with his rich fertilizing life behind me. William Faulkner said once that Keats's "Ode on a Grecian Urn" was worth any number of maiden aunts. In the first place there were no maiden aunts in Keats's way, so he didn't have to grind up any old ladies in his short gorgeous run. In the second place it's as nearly criminal a claim as any artist ever made; and if I should mouth anything so shameful, I hope somebody blots me out by sundown. That sort of talk makes me wish all art could vanish tonight to save the life of a single threatened child.

All I meant was, Rafe Noren's life enabled me. And now I've lived to say so. The fact that, in dancing, he sought people's eyes makes me hope that nothing here offends his ghost. Absorbed as he was, he knew people watched him. They were part of his goal—them, himself and the eye of God. What maker ever worked for more?

* * *

I'VE TRIED TO LAY OUT THE STORY WE MADE IN HIS LAST weeks, only one of the several tales he told in that short a life. Having come this far I've learned at least one usable fact. *You can leave me out.* It was childish selfishness to think till now that I harmed Rafe badly or caused his death. He had been flung down more times than one, before I knew him. He fed his own fire, he and people long before me and his destiny in general. He made that final killing climb for his own ample reasons, to fill his own needs. And he died in a place devoted to hope.

The thing that seems worth seeing from here is, Raphael Noren watched his life and changed his story in ways that kept it from closing in fear or waste. Didn't he end as a Ghost Dancer still, calling down peace with grave self-possession, alone but calm? How many old men can say as much? How many like me, who've plumbed the reaches of physical pleasure and heard the word *love* on many lips? So leave me out but, long as you can, recall his name and some kind of picture against the light—a boy becoming an actual eagle or the generous giver of fire and warmth or laughing his way through mortal trial, denying his fate a few more days.

ABOUT THE AUTHOR

Born in Macon, North Carolina, in 1933, Reynolds Price attended North Carolina schools and received his Bachelor of Arts degree from Duke University. As a Rhodes Scholar he studied for three years at Merton College, Oxford, receiving the Bachelor of Letters with a thesis on Milton. In 1958 he returned to Duke, where he is now James B. Duke Professor of English. His first novel A LONG AND HAPPY LIFE appeared in 1962 and received the William Faulkner Award. It was followed by THE NAMES AND FACES OF HEROES (a volume of stories); A GENEROUS MAN (a novel); LOVE AND WORK (a novel); PERMANENT ERRORS (stories); THINGS THEMSELVES (essays and scenes); THE SURFACE OF EARTH (a novel); EARLY DARK (a play); A PALPABLE GOD (translations from the Bible with an essay on the origins and life of narrative); THE SOURCE OF LIGHT (a novel); VITAL PROVISIONS (poems); PRIVATE CONTENTMENT (a play); KATE VAIDEN (a novel); THE LAWS OF ICE (poems); A COMMON ROOM: ESSAYS 1954–1987; GOOD HEARTS (a novel); CLEAR PICTURES (a memoir); THE TONGUES OF ANGELS (a novel); and THE USE OF FIRE (poems). In 1989 his trilogy of plays NEW MUSIC premiered at the Cleveland Play House and has now been published.

Reynolds Price is a member of the National Academy and Institute of Arts and Letters. His books have appeared in sixteen languages.